A Novel

THREE-FIFTHS

A Novel

THREE-FIFTHS

JOHN VERCHER

Copyright © 2019 by John Vercher
Cover and jacket design by 2Faced Design

ISBN 978-1-947993-67-9
ISBN 978-1-947993-82-2
Library of Congress Control Number: 2019945376

First hardcover edition September 2019 by Agora Books
An imprint of Polis Books, LLC
221 River St., 9th Fl., #9070
Hoboken, NJ 07030
www.PolisBooks.com

For Michelle, JJ, and Miles
You are my everything

CHAPTER
ONE

March, 1995

The dumpsters stunk of half-eaten food and the sweet sour of stale beer. Streetlamps lit snowflakes that hovered in the stillness like trapped fireflies. The cold air stiffened Bobby's lungs and he fought back a wheeze. He tucked his cigarette behind his ear, took a hit from his inhaler, then lit up. The sulfur from the match pierced his nose and made his eyes water. He wiped the blurriness away and saw through the fence surrounding the dock that someone was on the other side.

"Who the hell is that?" Bobby asked Luis.

Luis shrugged. Bobby moved closer, fingers through the chain link. A large white man sat on the edge of a red pickup bed, parked in the shadows between the streetlights. Thick arms wrapped around his knees, which were pulled into his chest.

Bobby and Luis traded nervous glances. He felt at the knot of cash in his pocket and gave Luis the once over. The scrawny fry cook

1

stood a head shorter than Bobby and a good twenty pounds lighter. No help there if whoever this guy was decided to make a move.

"You want to go back in through the front?" Bobby asked Luis.

"Nah, my car is parked back here. Whatever, man, don't be a pussy."

Bobby flashed his middle finger. *Fuck it, if* he *isn't scared...* He pushed and the gate creaked open. The man's head popped up. He jumped down from the bed of the truck.

Bobby and Luis both paused before they continued on, keeping their distance while trying to appear that they weren't. *Show no fear, but don't look at him, either.* He gave the guy a quick nod and watched from the corner of his eye as the stranger held his hands out, confused.

Luis and Bobby walked faster.

"Yo, Bobby," he said. "Where you going?"

Bobby slid to a stop. When he turned, his mouth fell open and his cigarette stuck to the inside of his lip. Aaron had shaved his head completely. His pale arms were covered in tattoos, their designs obscured in the darkness. He sparked his lighter and the flame illuminated his face, revealing a topography of violence past. A raised scar ran across the bottom of his eye, another on his lip curved up towards his nose. Bobby wanted to look away, but instead squinted for a better look. Aaron snapped the lighter shut, throwing his face back into the shadows.

"Holy shit," Bobby said. "Look at this Hulked-out motherfucker."

Aaron smiled a mouthful of large, bright-white teeth. Bobby jerked his chin back in surprise. Aaron tightened his smile, covering them with his lips.

"Get your narrow ass over here," Aaron said. He held his arms out and Bobby walked into Aaron's tight embrace. Bobby gave him a couple of hard slaps to the back to get him to let go but Aaron squeezed harder. He stunk of beer and body odor. Aaron kissed the top of his head. Bobby pulled away and Aaron looked him in the eyes.

"I missed you, man," he said.

"All right, all right," Bobby said. He pushed Aaron off and laughed. "Let go of me, you queer."

"Hey, fuck off with that shit," Aaron said. He gave Bobby a playful shove. Bobby caught a look behind Aaron's half-hearted smile and remembered that first day in the visitor's center. *Stupid.* He opened his mouth to apologize when Luis called to him from the open driver's side door of his car.

"Bobby! See you tomorrow?"

Bobby gave a dismissive wave. Luis sucked his teeth and got in. Aaron took unsteady steps back to his truck where an empty six-pack container sat next to another half-empty one in the bed. Aaron sat on the edge and traced the toe of his boot in the snow. Bobby sat next to him as Luis drove off.

"Hanging with the beaners, now?" Aaron said.

"Luis? He's okay," Bobby said. He elbowed Aaron in the arm. "One of the good ones, you know?"

"Uh huh."

Bobby stopped smiling. Aaron winked at him and elbowed him back.

"Three years!" Bobby shouted, and smacked him on the shoulder. "Jesus, kid, it's good to see you."

Aaron laughed and reached back to hand Bobby a beer. He pushed it back towards him. "Still, huh?" he asked. Bobby nodded. "You're of age now, man, and we didn't even get to celebrate."

"I'm good, man. You know that."

"Come on, one won't kill you. Three years, you said it yourself. How many times do I get out of prison?"

"Hopefully just this once."

"Exactly. So throw one back with me, huh? Besides, alcoholism isn't genetic, man."

"Are you retarded? Yes, it is."

"Really? How about that."

Aaron chugged his beer and sent the empty sailing into the lower parking lot where it shattered into musical shards. Now under the streetlight, Bobby studied Aaron's face. His nose looked like it'd been broken more than once and the scar under his eye looked raised and swollen, as if someone had stitched it together with barbed wire. There was something more than the physical damage to his face. A veneer of sadness, of pained and disingenuous smiles. He picked at the label on a fresh bottle. Bobby squeezed his shoulder and gave him a shake.

"You all right, kid?" Bobby asked.

"Don't I look it?" Another tight smile.

Bobby shrugged. "Eh. Kind of." He patted the truck. "This is a beauty, by the way."

"The old man had it waiting for me. A welcome home present."

"That's a hell of a present."

"Said I earned it."

They laughed. Aaron hadn't earned much of anything as long as they'd known each other. His father was an investment banker and a major donor to the campaigns of local government officials. Father and son took great advantage of the resulting perks. Speeding tickets disappeared. Arrests for shoplifting comic books erased from permanent records.

Then possession with intent to distribute. A third strike. And he had mouthed off to the judge. Long, hard time awaited.

And yet, only three years. Membership had its benefits.

"Look, I'm happy to see you and all, but it's fucking freezing out here. Let's go somewhere, and give me them keys because you're already wrecked."

"Just a couple more minutes, all right?" Aaron pleaded. "I've been indoors for over a thousand days. This air feels so good, man. Even when they let us in the yard, the air there felt different. Like when it passed through the fence, it got dirty." He brushed snow off the side rail of the truck bed. "This thing felt like a coffin on the way over here. Hell, you want it? You can have it."

A few of the guys in the kitchen were on work release or parole. Russell, the general manager, had done time when he was younger. He often told the story of how he made it, how he got out, and how he wouldn't let them make the same mistakes twice. "You have to understand that this system is designed to keep you young bucks in it. Once you got that label, that prison stink on you? You never really have a shot after that. Especially not when you look like us. They'll look for any reason to put you back inside. Can't pay your court fees because that job keeping the walk-in clean only pays minimum wage? Back in. Get caught hanging with one of your homies who caught a charge, too? Back in. You young brothers have less than half a chance. People will talk to you about accountability, tell you that you have none. That you have a commitment to that life. If you keep going back in, that might end up being the case. If you're in long enough, if the things that happen to you are bad enough, you don't know what to do with yourself on the outside, that even though you tell yourself differently, that there's no way you ever want to go back, it's becomes the only home you know."

Bobby never bought it, the system being out to get them. Invariably, the cops would show up and haul one of Russell's pet projects out the front door, leaving Russell standing in the doorway, shaking his head. But as Bobby sat on the edge of that truck and watched Aaron chew at his nails, some of what Russell said resonated. Aaron was no long-timer, but the life he'd led before prison had been easy. Problems of his own making disappeared with a phone call from his father to the right people. Maybe now, back in the world, Aaron realized he had gotten used to the dirty air of incarceration. Maybe that world, in some way, held more comfort for him than this one. It seemed so irrational and yet there it was.

Bobby shrugged off the thought and held his hand out for the keys. They climbed into the truck. When Bobby reached down to adjust his seat, his hand brushed against something rough. He pulled out a brick, broken at the edges.

"They teach you masonry in the joint?" Bobby forced a laugh, but Aaron didn't smile. He took the brick from Bobby and set it on the floor next to his beers. "Seriously. What's that for?"

"You remember that little mini-bat I used to keep under my seat in case shit went sideways?" Bobby nodded. "There was a pile of these broken bricks by a dumpster outside the prison so I grabbed one. Not everyone out here is going to be as happy as you are to see me."

"Yeah, all right, I get it, I guess. But a brick?"

"Until I get a gun, yeah."

"O-kay, tough guy" Bobby said. He laughed, but Aaron remained silent. They shut the doors and Bobby started the truck. Aaron pulled his knees into his chest. The tight space in the truck made him turtle in on himself. For all of his new bulk, inked skin, and scars, he was an anxious mess. He was scared.

"Man, you weren't kidding, huh? You sure you're all right?"

Aaron reached for the radio. Bobby felt the inside of his ears tense, steeling himself for the bass heavy hip-hop Aaron loved to torture him with whenever he drove him to school.

Instead, classical music filtered through the speakers. Aaron let his knees go. He stopped gnawing at his nails and relaxed into his seat. Bobby flashed him a side-eye. Aaron laughed.

"Okay, okay," he said.

"Look, if there's something you need to tell me…" Bobby said.

"Take it easy. There's a reason, I swear."

"I can't wait to hear this."

Bobby shook his head and pulled the truck out onto McKnight Road. The light dusting of snow slithered back and forth on the street behind the cars in front of them like phantom snakes, and the heat of the defroster made the wipers drag and groan across the windshield. They stopped at a traffic light and the piece ended. The public radio station delivered a newsbreak.

"I'm so sick of this trial," Bobby said. "I don't even have a television and I still can't get away from it." Aaron gave a little laugh but kept staring out his window. "I mean, you should hear the guys in the kitchen, just swearing he's not guilty. Like they win something if he's found innocent. It's fucking crazy." Bobby watched Aaron for a response, but nothing. "Oh, *now* you go quiet? You better say something, because right now I feel like you're going to like flip out and murder me, like Colonel Mustard, with a brick, in the red pickup."

Aaron turned to face him and squinted. "You think I'd hurt you?"

"No, no, I'm kidding. Kind of. You're just kind of hammered already, which is cool, you should be, totally, but we're listening to this sad old bastard music and you got arms as big as my legs and you don't even talk like you used to like you used to and, fuck, man, I don't know what to think."

"How did I talk before?"

"Come off it, man, that wannabe wigger shit. You know."

"Yeah, I know," he said. He puffed his cheeks and breathed out through pursed lips. "Okay, so the music. I got a library detail when I first went in. You remember how skinny I was. After–"

He stopped. Bobby glanced away from the road and towards Aaron. Headlights from a car in the opposite lane illuminated his face. His wet eyes glistened.

"After it happened, they thought I'd be safer working there. There was this section where you could actually listen to CDs. Nothing but classical, though. Nothing aggressive. No metal. Definitely no rap. But then I read in one of the books there—"

"They got you to read? Maybe this wasn't so bad for you after all," Bobby said, smacking him on the shoulder. Aaron didn't return his smile and Bobby cleared his throat.

"I found out that a bunch of this shit actually caused riots the first time they played them. That's a trip, right?"

Something new in his voice, an almost imperceptible crack, a slight waver, made Bobby not like where this story was headed. He nodded to answer Aaron's question and longed for the quiet about which he had just complained.

"What was I going to do?" Aaron asked. "I was just this kid, scared shitless. I never slept, and even when I'd start to pass out from exhaustion, the slightest sound made me jump. So I'd find a corner in the library stacks and just listen over and over again until I had to go back to my cell. And I waited for the end of the week when I'd see you." He started to fidget again and cracked open another beer. He finished in five fast swallows.

"It didn't take me long to memorize the movements of the pieces. Ten thousand repetitions, right? I must have doubled that. I started to hum the songs to myself to fall asleep. The first night it worked, the night I got my first hour of undisturbed sleep, it was the night before you visited," he said.

He stopped. He twisted his hands around his beer bottle like a wet rag. "It was just a beating the first time. That's what got me the library duty. The night before you visited, Bobby, I tried to fight him, I promise you I did, but he was so strong. He bashed my head my against the wall of the cell and my body wouldn't cooperate anymore. At least not with me. All I could do was try to make the music loud

8

enough in my head to drown out the sounds. It didn't work.

"Later in the infirmary, it did, though. While they stitched me up, my brain kept trying to make me relive what he did to me, kept repeating how he told me that this was just the start, that the others would have their turn after he broke me in. So I hummed while the doc went to work on me. I remember how she looked at me, like, how could I be humming after all of that. It was the only thing that kept me from opening my wrists up with the teeth I had left."

Bobby curled his hands around the steering wheel and blinked away the burning in his eyes. He could not shake the vivid image of Aaron's violation. He remembered Aaron on the other side of the visitor's window, just hours separated from the incident, and now he understood why Aaron had never wanted him to return. They had broken far more than his face.

"Aaron," Bobby said. "I'm so sorry."

"Did you put me in that cell?" Bobby shook his head. "Then don't be sorry." Aaron turned to look out his window again and Bobby reached for his shoulder, but pulled back, not sure why he had done either.

Aaron shook it off and slapped his cheeks. "Sucked they didn't have any comics in the library," Aaron said with a belch. "You got a lot to catch me up on. But they kept me on library detail and I did read. Just fiction and stuff at first. Anything to get out of my head, you know? But then I got some assignments. I had to start reading language, world history, all kinds of stuff."

"Assignments?" Bobby asked. "What do you mean?"

"Your last name means 'of a swarthy complexion' in Sicilian," Aaron said. "Did you know that?"

What the hell did Aaron mean? Who gave him an assignment?

Aaron cracked his last beer. Bobby accelerated.

The truck hurtled past Duquesne and Bobby glanced across the river to the Incline. The tracks were lit by a row of white bulbs on each side. None of this fit. Bobby envisioned the day Aaron would get out countless times, but when he did, he'd had a different scene altogether in his head. They'd fall right back into their old rhythm. Bobby would make fun of DC comics. Aaron would make fun of Marvel. They'd revel in their mutual hatred of Image. Bobby would bitch at Aaron for his shitty taste in music. Aaron would make fun of Bobby's shitty clothes. They'd compare shitty family lives. They'd have three years back. Instant happiness, just add water.

They joked, they laughed but it was hollow, wrong. Aaron was different and it went beyond physical change, the bulking up. That much made sense. Even beyond the music, the tattoos and the way he talked, something hovered that dimmed the light that used to radiate from him. His smiles, tight. As though they weren't allowed.

Bobby had to change that. No matter what had happened to him, his best friend was home. Aaron still needed his help, but not like when they were kids. This was different. Bobby didn't know if he could fix this. They hit Forbes Avenue. The Cathedral of Learning stood a beacon in the distance.

"Where are we going, anyway?" Bobby asked.

"Oh shit, yeah, North Oakland," he said. "Got someone I need to meet up with tonight."

"Just got out and you're back at it already?"

"No, it's not like that. I promised somebody I'd check in on someone. Stay with him for a bit."

"I get it, hanging with me and my mom in Homewood's going to cramp your style. I'll give it to you, a cell would seem like a resort in comparison." Aaron laughed. "So what do you want to do, man? We don't have to go there just yet, right? You're out!"

"I'm fucking starving," he said. "Oh, shit. Let's hit the dirty 'O.'"

Bobby groaned. Aaron knew he hated the Original Hot Dog

Shop. It was the only place open after the bars let out. Drunken college kids and the gangbangers from the nearby neighborhoods swarmed for forties, five-dollar pizzas, and bags of greasy fries as big as a grown man's head. But the streets of Oakland were near empty. The college kids had gone home for spring break. It was the last place he wanted to go, but Aaron seemed so excited. He had always lived for their food, especially drunk, which he was, and Bobby imagined how good it might taste for him tonight of all nights.

"Fuck. Okay."

"Really?" Aaron asked.

"I know I'm going to regret it, but yeah, let's do it. You said it yourself, how many times is my best friend going to get out of prison? Those fries are going to mess up your new girlish figure, though."

"Fucking A," he said. The smile now big, his eyes tight and bright.

Bobby parked on Bouquet less than a half block back from the corner where the "O" sat. Light from the neon sign filled the truck and bathed them both in red. Aaron opened his door, but Bobby stayed put.

"What are you doing?" Aaron asked.

"It's freezing," Bobby said. "Get what you want, I'll keep the truck running."

"Okay. While I'm in there, I'll see if they have pads in the bathroom for your vagina."

"Oh, fuck you, man," Bobby forced another laugh and turned off the engine.

"Atta boy."

The air inside tasted like the bathrooms looked to Bobby. As much as he wanted to do this for Aaron, his Spider-sense tingled and he wanted to go back to the truck even more. Then he saw why.

Two young black men sat at a table near the counter. One had his head down and looked passed out, an almost empty forty at his

11

elbow. He wore a blue stocking cap, and a thick blue flannel coat, a uniform Bobby knew far too well in Homewood. The other heaped fries into his mouth and sucked down pop from a plastic 32-ounce cup. No colors on him. Only a tan sweatshirt with a lined hood and dark blue jeans. He looked younger than both Bobby and Aaron, but he eyed the two of them hard as soon as they walked in. Under the fluorescent lights Bobby saw clearly for the first time that night what doubtless the kid did as well.

Aaron's tattoos.

Double lightning bolts on his shoulders. An Iron Eagle where his collar bones met.

Spiderwebs on both elbows.

"Jesus," Bobby whispered to himself.

Bobby stood behind Aaron as he ordered at the register. He heard the kid at the table suck his teeth in disgust.

"Some mark-ass busters up in this piece tonight," he said. Bobby pretended not to hear and stole what he thought was a surreptitious look over his shoulder. The kid met his eyes before Bobby spun his head forward again. "Yeah, you hear me talking," he said.

Bobby stared at Aaron's wide back. Aaron either didn't hear or didn't care and continued to place their order.

"Where you get them spiderwebs, huh?" the kid asked Aaron. "In the joint, right? Guess you a hard rock."

Aaron turned around to look at Bobby and smiled.

Don't smile, please don't smile. Why the fuck are you smiling?

He slapped Bobby on the stomach with the back of his hand.

"Got to piss," he said. "Be right back."

"What? No," he said. "Don't leave, don't leave, don't leave—" but Aaron walked off. The old man behind the counter scooped floppy fries into a white bag until it wouldn't close, dotting it with translucent grease spots. Bobby darted quick glances over his shoulder to see if the kid was still watching.

He was. His boy next to him remained half-conscious, but stirred. Aaron came back from the bathroom as the old man slid the pizza and fries across the counter.

"We good? Can we go now?" Bobby said.

"What, we're not gonna eat here?"

"What?"

"Relax," Aaron said. "Pay and let's go."

"Very funny," Bobby said as he slid his money across the counter.

"Bitch ass motherfucker," the kid said to Aaron.

Aaron laughed. A chair scraped against the floor. The kid was right behind them. He was taller than Aaron, but slender. His face was lean, the skin pulled tight on the bone beneath.

Bobby's heart pounded and he felt the familiar pressure of an approaching asthma attack filling up the spaces in his chest.

"I say something funny?" the kid said to the back of Aaron's head. Aaron turned, food in hand and looked up at the kid. "What?" the kid said. "Yeah, I know what those tattoos mean, and no, I'm not scared of you. Y'all lucky my boy sleeping." He popped his shoulders at Aaron.

Aaron didn't flinch and smiled at him.

"Excuse us, please," Aaron said. He sidestepped the kid and Bobby followed close behind. *Thank Christ.* They headed for the door.

"That's what I thought," the kid said. "Get the hell up out of here."

So close. They were almost out.

Aaron's hand was on the handle. He let go and turned back to the dining room. He put his tongue inside his upper lip and made monkey noises while he gave the kid the finger. Bobby pushed him out, but he already heard the footsteps behind them.

Aaron walked and Bobby shoved him again to rush him towards the truck. He took a few running steps then slowed again while he pushed a handful of fries into his mouth. The door of the "O" flung open and slammed off the wall.

"You got jokes, huh?" the kid shouted. He ran at them. Bobby tried to take off but the sidewalk was slippery and he nearly fell. The kid caught up to him and grabbed the collar of Bobby's jacket. Bobby yelled for Aaron, who now was running for the truck. Bobby panicked at Aaron's sudden cowardice, frightened that he'd leave him to get pummeled or worse. Bobby pulled free of the kid's grasp and bolted for the driver's side of the truck. He jumped in and swung the door shut. The kid pounded on his window. Bobby started the truck, ready to floor it when he turned and saw Aaron wasn't there, just the pizza box and fries spilled out across the seat. He looked up to see Aaron cross in front of the headlights, heading for the kid. The kid backed away from Bobby's window, and he saw him motion for Aaron to bring it on. Bobby yelled for Aaron to stop. To come back and get in the truck. Then he saw the brick in his hand.

Brick cracked bone and the kid collapsed, a marionette with cut strings. Bobby heard his head smack against the sidewalk. He grasped the door, breath fogging the window. He pulled back to wipe away the haze.

Deep lines cleaved the flesh of the boy's face, bloodless, until his mouth opened, gaping and silent. Then blood poured out of every cut. His boots churned the snow to dirty slush as he writhed. He moaned, quietly at first, then louder like an approaching siren. His arms trembled as he tried desperately to push himself up from the pavement. Bobby went to open his door, but he had locked it in his panic. As he found the switch and pulled on the handle, Aaron threw open the passenger door. Bobby jumped. Aaron dropped his brick on the floor in front of him.

"Go, go, go," he said.

Aaron was breathing hard, but his voice was calm. His breath stunk of beer. Bobby forgot he'd already started the truck and the engine's insides scraped when he turned the key again.

The tires screeched as he took the corner onto Forbes Avenue. Aaron squeezed Bobby's knee. "Slow down."

Aaron craned to look out the rear window while Bobby watched the rearview. The police station across the street often kept an empty patrol car parked outside as a deterrent. As they passed, the car didn't move. No lights. No sirens. Bobby took a last look back and saw the door of the Original open before the neon lights disappeared from view.

"Jesus, Aaron what the fuck did you do?" Bobby said. His breaths got shorter and his chest tingled, his asthma forming an iron maiden around his airways, the spikes poking at his lungs. The deeper he tried to inhale, the harder it got to take another breath. He wheezed, reached inside his front jacket pocket and grabbed his inhaler, but dropped it on the floor. Aaron picked it up and held it out to him. The blood on his fingers smeared on the plastic case and Bobby wondered if it was Aaron's or the kid's. He stared at the inhaler in Aaron's outstretched hand. Aaron saw the blood and wiped it off with the hem of his white ribbed tank top.

"Shit," he said. "Sorry. Fuck, I got it on your pants, too."

When he handed it back, the periphery of Bobby's vision had already begun to blacken. He snatched it and took a deep puff. Aaron popped open the glove compartment and grabbed a pack of smokes. He held one out for Bobby while he pushed the lighter in on the console. Bobby reached for it and pinched it between his dried lips.

"Fuck, man," Bobby said. "What did you do? What did you *do*?"

"You're going to miss the turn. Up here."

The lighter popped. Aaron and Bobby reached for it at the same time but Aaron let him take it. Maybe if he jammed it into Aaron's cheek, or better yet his eye, something soft and painful, whatever would give him enough time to get away, he'd jump out of the truck and let it swerve into a pole while he ran off into the night. He could hide out in St. Paul's Cathedral and call the police.

And tell them what?

Tell them he took off and left some kid for dead, and by the way, the maniac that did it, he was too drunk to drive himself away from the scene of the crime, so guess who took care of that for him? They'd lock him up, too and he'd end up looking like Aaron did the day he went to visit him or worse yet, he'd get his skull smashed to shit like that kid he just left back there squirming on the sidewalk.

That kid. Jesus, that was someone's kid. Eighteen. Nineteen, maybe? Wouldn't see his next birthday. Probably wouldn't see tomorrow.

Bobby imagined the boy's mother. The police knocking on her door to tell her someone had caved her son's head in with a brick and left him to die on the street. He thought of his own mother, Isabel, imagined her wails of grief, but all he could hear were the boy's moans. Both her imagined cries and the boy's real ones sounded like "why."

"You missed it," Aaron said. Bobby blinked back a tear. "Take the next left."

The lighter wobbled as Bobby brought it to the tip of his cigarette. Aaron wrapped his fingers around Bobby's hand to hold it still. Bobby felt the heat of the orange coil on his lips, breathed in the toasted tobacco as the end sizzled. His lungs felt stiff from the asthma attack and he hacked until he nearly gagged. He was grateful. It provided an excuse for the tears that rolled down his cheeks. Aaron wiped one away with a calloused thumb. Bobby smacked his hand.

"Get the fuck off me," he said.

Aaron held his hands up in surrender, then gently took the lighter from Bobby's hand. He lit up and cracked his window. Cold air leaked in as the smoke sucked out. He slid down in the seat and thumped a boot up on the dash. Aaron might have killed the kid, yet he reclined in his seat in a near post-coital glow. The Aaron Bobby knew, or rather the one he thought he knew, couldn't have gotten laid if he paid for it. Buzzard-necked Aaron, a buck-thirty if he was a pound. Aaron, Bobby's fellow comic-book nerd. His best friend, Aaron the wannabe. Aaron the wigger.

Something had taken his place. His name. A pale imitation of his personality. Not him. A shaved head and combat boots with red laces replaced the baggy jeans and shell-top Adidas tennis shoes. The once-scrawny neck disappeared into his mountainous shoulders. Each time Bobby glanced at Aaron he tried to picture the boy he knew before he got locked up, hoped every blink would bring him out of some fever dream, sweating under the comforter, huddled up on his couch, but all he saw was that black kid's face smashed to hell and his stomach turned.

"Hang a right," Aaron said.

"Why?" Bobby asked.

Aaron looked at Bobby with genuine confusion. "Because it's the way to get to the apartment?" he asked.

"You're joking right now? You know what I mean! Why the fuck did you do that to that kid?"

"Why? That kid grabbed you, and you're asking me why? How many times, Bobby?" he asked. His upper lip pulled back from his teeth. "How many times did you have to save my ass from those fucking monkeys in high school? In the bathroom? In the parking lot? You remember that? Did you think I'd let that happen to you? Because it was about to."

"I know, but—"

"But nothing. Jesus, dude, you told me yourself, over and over again. You remember that? I didn't listen then, but I learned my lesson." He blew out a cloud of smoke and leaned on the console next to Bobby, almost daring him to make eye contact. He cocked his head back towards the rear of the truck, gesturing to where they'd left the kid. "They're animals, Bobby. And some animals need to be put down."

Bobby felt his face go flush. As he pulled on the wheel to make the turn, he remembered a different street.

An alleyway, the one behind his Grandpap's.

His first fight, one he'd never forget, a story he'd never shared with Aaron, or anyone else. His face recalled the sting in his cheek, the way his own blood tasted like a penny in his mouth.

He had been eleven years old.

It was the first time he'd ever said the word "nigger."

The same day his mother had told him he was one.

CHAPTER TWO

Aaron directed them to a dilapidated apartment building in North Oakland. He opened his door to get out, but Bobby stayed. He gripped the steering wheel and bounced his forehead against it. The smell of greasy fries and pizza filled the cab and made him more nauseated. When Aaron got out, he'd floor it, drive to the police station and turn himself and Aaron in.

But it was Aaron's truck, and he had driven away from the scene of a crime.

I left that kid there to die.

A tear spattered on his leg where Aaron's hand had left a bloody fingerprint when he'd squeezed his knee. Aaron closed his door.

"Look, I'm sorry," Aaron said. "I didn't plan for that to happen."

"You killed him, Aaron. You fucking killed him."

"What did you want me to do? He was coming after *you*."

"Because of *you*."

"Oh, come on, man. That was nothing. He didn't have to step to us like that."

Bobby turned, his forehead still pressed to the steering wheel, and squinted at Aaron through bleary eyes. "What is wrong with you?" he asked.

"What if he'd had a gun, Bobby? You think of that?"

"He was a kid, Aaron. Just a punk kid."

"And nobody's going to give a shit. You know what, man. This is the same bullshit from high school. You don't appreciate shit, and you're starting to piss me off. Let's go. Grab the food. I'm fucking starving."

Aaron jumped out of the truck slammed the door shut behind him. Bobby flinched, and peeled his forehead away from the steering wheel. He took measured breaths and rationalized. How would he explain his part in this? It wasn't his truck, but Aaron was drunk. Aaron forced him into this. But he didn't even have a gun, a knife, anything that would make the cops believe he'd threatened Bobby into cooperating. Aaron tapped on the glass and shouted a muffled "let's go." Bobby knew there had to be a way out of this, but not now. He'd provoked Aaron without even meaning to, and if he even began to suspect that Bobby might turn them in, who was to say he wouldn't end up like the kid?

Wait a minute. This is the same kid who barely broke one-hundred and thirty pounds with his clothes soaking wet. I'm afraid of him?

But he was. He was terrified. He grabbed the pizza and fries and followed.

The third floor hallway of the building reeked of weed. A bass-heavy rap track bounced off the cracked plaster walls. The source of everything was a door at the end of the hall. Bobby tilted his head at Aaron, curious as to their destination. Aaron slapped at the door with his open palm. Nothing. He cursed under his breath and pounded.

The music quieted. The pinhole of light in the fisheye went black. A chain slid. The deadbolt clicked.

A baby-faced white kid with close-cropped blond hair, no older than the one they'd left in the street, opened the door. He slapped hands with Aaron, then pulled him in for a half-hug. He had to go up on his toes to reach Aaron's broad shoulders. He wore a long basketball jersey over camouflage pants tucked into a pair of Docs with red laces, just like Aaron's. When he thumped Aaron on the back, Bobby saw a swastika on the back of his hand and felt what was becoming an all-too familiar lump in his throat return. The young skinhead eyed Bobby standing in the doorway holding the pizza and fries like some kind of lost delivery boy.

"Who's the guinea?" he asked Aaron.

"Easy, Cort," Aaron replied. "It's Cort, right?" The kid nodded. "He's cool."

Cort nodded toward the living room and signaled for Bobby to enter. He grabbed the pizza from Bobby and immediately helped himself to a limp slice, dangling it over his open mouth as he dropped down on the puke green couch. A .45 sat next to a four-footer on the glass coffee table in front of him. Aaron pointed at the gun.

"That me?" he asked.

Cort nodded and took a deep hit from the bong. Aaron picked up the gun and inspected it before he tucked it in the back of his waistband as if it was something he'd always done. He pulled back the blinds from a window and peered down into the street. Cort exhaled a cloud of smoke and coughed fitfully as he turned the volume back up on the episode of *Yo! MTV Raps*. Aaron turned and glared at him.

"The fuck you looking at, yo?" Cort asked.

"Yo?" Aaron said, then laughed, disgusted. "What do you think your uncle Hank would say if he heard you talking that nonsense? Caught you watching this garbage?"

"Yeah, well, his dumb-ass is still locked up isn't he? So he ain't saying shit."

Aaron walked to the couch and stood over Cort.

"Say something smart about him again." Aaron reached behind his back and gripped the gun. "Go on."

"Aaron, Jesus," Bobby said, the words a whisper, strangled by the desert in his throat.

Cort looked up at Aaron, then over to Bobby who shook his head at him. His tough façade folded in on itself. "Yeah, all right, man," Cort said. "My bad...I mean, it's cool."

"Good." Aaron said. "Turn this shit off and point me to the head." Cort gestured. Bobby watched as Aaron's heavy boots thumped down a short hallway and disappeared into a room off to the right.

"Whatever, man," Cort mumbled to himself when Aaron was out of earshot.

The gun-like sound effects of an MTV news brief exploded from the television behind Bobby and startled him. Tabitha Soren recounted the day's proceedings in the O.J. trial. Detective Furhman had been questioned about using racial slurs on the job as the attorneys for the defense attempted to build a case for a conspiracy. The skinhead shook his head and sneered. He punched Bobby in the thigh.

"You believe this shit?" he asked. "No way he didn't do it. Look at his eyes. They got no whites in them, just blackness. Like a...like..." He stared at the screen, heavy-lidded. Bobby leaned forward to see if he'd nodded off, then offered an end to his sentence.

"A shark?" Bobby asked.

Cort's eyes widened and he snapped his fingers at Bobby. "Oh, shit, yeah, that's good. I was thinking chimp, but a shark. Shit, yeah. Anyway, I hope they still do hangings in Cali. Am I right?"

Bobby's feet felt like they didn't belong to him, then his hands, his arms, his legs. He couldn't feel his face. For a minute, it seemed as if he wasn't really there. Maybe he wasn't. Maybe he'd skidded out in the snow and crashed and none of this was happening. In fact, right now, he could be in a hospital bed while his comatose brain constructed the entire thing. No attempted murder. No accessory to attempted murder. Just brain dead. The heavy bass thumped from the television again. Cort bobbed his head and mouthed the lyrics to Biggie Small's "Warning", then looked over his shoulder down the hall where Aaron had gone and turned the volume down low again. Feeling came back to Bobby's limbs in a rush and he walked down the hall after Aaron as bong water bubbled behind him.

Aaron rinsed lather from his hands. The drain was slow and the water turned into a red and white soup before getting sucked down. Aaron inspected his fingernails. Bobby hadn't noticed before how long they were. He remembered seeing some show where inmates grew them long and filed them to points and he caught a chill.

"You all right?" Aaron asked.

"Where are we? Who is that guy?"

Aaron hissed through his teeth. "That punk. No dignity. It's for his uncle I don't beat his fucking ass. I owe him that. That's why I'm staying with him for a bit."

"What do you owe his uncle?" Bobby asked. Though he wanted to know, he dreaded the answer.

"Nothing. Everything," Aaron answered. "All depends on who asks. He brought me into the brotherhood. Kept me safe."

"The brotherhood?" Bobby said, his voice raised. "Do you hear yourself? I don't believe this. Who am I even talking to? I have to get the fuck out of here."

"And go where, Bobby?"

Aaron splashed water on his face and looked for a towel but none hung on the bar. When he grabbed the hem of his shirt to pull it to

23

his face, he noticed the smeared blood that he'd wiped from Bobby's inhaler. He took off his shirt, and dried his face with a clean spot. His chest and back were covered in acne and Bobby guessed someone inside found a way to get him steroids. He turned around to piss. "88" was tattooed on both shoulder blades. In between the zits on his back were round scars, the raised flesh the circumference of the business end of a cigarette. Someone had used him for an ashtray.

When he turned around, Bobby's eyes went to the large swastika on his sternum, the arms of the broken cross bending across his chest. Bobby backed up as Aaron walked towards him until he bumped against the wall in the tight hallway. Aaron leaned against the doorframe. His face softened.

"Look, I'm sorry I flipped out downstairs. I know you're scared, but you're safe here," he said. "You're always safe when I'm around. I owe you at least that much. We'll get some rest and figure things out in the morning. I promise you, everything will be fine. Now go grab the pizza before that little shit eats it all." Bobby opened his mouth to protest but Aaron patted him on the cheek, squeezed past him and walked to another door at the end of the hallway.

For an instant, Bobby was furious, far more angry than scared. When Aaron touched his cheek, Bobby wanted to reach out and grab him by his neck and scream in his face. He wanted to squeeze until he found the huge Adam's apple that used to bob up and down in the scrawny neck of the kid Bobby always had to talk down from his perpetual state of weed-fueled paranoia. It had never been the other way around. Sure Aaron was drunk, but below all that freaky calm had to be that same kid in a panic.

But he wasn't there. His eyes looked as cold as their ice-blue hue. He'd been out less than twenty-four hours and he damn near killed someone. Now he wanted pizza. Prison had created Prison Aaron and Prison Aaron did what he thought he had to do, supposedly to

24

protect them both. Either he enjoyed it, didn't care that he'd go back if they were caught, or some twisted version of the two. The thought made Bobby go right back to being scared shitless.

Bobby walked back down the hall. Was there a phone in this dump? He should call Isabel. He spied one on the wall in the kitchen off the living room and stepped towards it, then stopped.

Aaron was right. Where would he go? What would he say? What could Isabel do?

He imagined the kid's mother again and pizza was the last thing he wanted. He went back to tell Aaron to get the fucking pizza himself, but Aaron had sprawled out on a single bed in the room at the end of the hall, out cold. Maybe he actually was scared, and putting on a front had exhausted him. Or maybe he was drunker than Bobby first thought and he just passed out. Bobby stood at the foot of the bed and stared, then let his eyes relax, like he did with the three-dimensional pictures he'd seen in the mall that are supposed to turn into dolphins. He wasn't sure why he looked at Aaron that way just then, nor did he know what he expected to see. He never saw the images they told him he was supposed to see in the pictures, either. They just gave him a headache.

Three years ago, Bobby had waited for more than thirty minutes to see Aaron. It had been his first week in prison. The line for visitors was long, and stunk of a mix of different perfumes and body sprays that smelled like the shit Isabel wore when she went out for the night. When Bobby saw no other guys there, he had worried that they might think he and Aaron were a couple, and he felt guilty about what that meant people thought about *him*, not what it might mean for Aaron. Guilty or not, selfish or not, the feeling compelled him to leave, but just as he had turned, an officer filed them all through the metal detectors and led them to the visitor's booths.

A moderately attractive woman sat next to Bobby. His knees bounced on the bottom of the counter. She stared, and he knew, just knew that she wondered, too, what a guy was doing visiting another guy at a men's prison. Bobby wrapped the phone cord around his thumb until the tip went red. The thick safety glass had handprints. Fingerprints. Grey lipstick smudges. He wondered if the woman next to him would kiss the glass, or try to touch hands through it, maybe whip out a tit and smush it against the Plexiglas while her man pressed his palm to it. Bobby noticed his own palms were wet. He didn't know why he was so nervous. Aaron had only been in a week. He'd be fine. Then the steel door squealed open and a guard led Aaron in by his bony elbow, swimming in his orange jumpsuit, head bowed, limping.

One eye was purple and swollen shut. A chain of small bruises ran around his neck and a zipper of stitches went down the side of his head where they had pulled out some of his hair. He shuffled to the window and went to sit but couldn't. His ass hovered until his legs shook. He pressed his bloated lips together and beads of sweat bloomed on his forehead with the effort. He gave up and leaned one knee on the stool as they both reached for the phones.

"Hey, man," Bobby said.

A tear ran out of Aaron's good eye.

"Don't ever come back here," he said.

The words came out soft and wet. His front teeth were gone. He hung up and shuffled back to the guard. Bobby called out after him and before he realized what he was doing, he pressed his palm against the glass. He noticed the woman next to him, staring. Bobby looked past her to see her man, who looked over his shoulder at Aaron. He snatched his hand away with the realization he might have just earned him another round of what he'd gotten before. The door slammed shut. Bobby stared at it until his eyes relaxed and his focus fell on his own greasy handprint, indiscriminate from the other remnants of futile attempts to connect, save its newness. He wiped the print away with his sleeve and left.

Bobby tried to go back once, but he wasn't on the list after that day. Or any of the days that followed.

Letters went unanswered. Days turned into months. Three years. A chunk of time that seemed like forever and not that long at the same time. Enough for the edges of what someone looked like to blur, even if only a little. Enough time that Bobby thought he remembered exactly what Aaron's voice sounded like but, after a while, didn't quite trust the memory. Just enough that when he saw Aaron in the parking lot for the first time after all those years, he had walked right past him.

Aaron snored. Bobby snuck across the room and pulled back the blinds on the window, looking out into the street as Aaron had, presumably looking for the same thing. But no cop cars patrolled the streets. No cars at all. The snow had piled up quickly and Bobby couldn't make out the street from the sidewalk. He walked to the front of the bed and curled up on the floor.

When Bobby was seven or eight, the teacher had told them a week or so ahead of time that the book fair was coming to school. His mother would only give him enough money to buy school lunch, but when the book fair came around, Bobby would eat as little as he could stand that week and would look for spare change all over the apartment. He would get so excited when the truck pulled up and unloaded their rolling folding metal shelves.

He always went straight for the *Choose Your Own Adventure* books. He only ever had enough money for one, maybe two, books but those were like having four or five books in one, *if* he made the right choices. They were fantasy books full of rainbow dragons and dark knights.

Do you go into a dark cave with only a torch or do you go around it and climb the mountain path with all assortments of evil monsters? Bobby picked the cave. They never said anything about monsters being in there so he thought he was safe.

The cave ended up killing him. It sucked, but then he got to start all over again.

The adrenaline finally ran out and exhaustion set in. Bobby's eyelids felt weighted. As he fell asleep, he envisioned a page to which he'd turned where he had to make a decision.

Choose your own adventure. If you want your skinhead best friend to confront a gang member, turn the page to see what happens next. If you want to drive on to the next destination and not watch him kill someone, turn to page ninety-three.

CHAPTER
THREE

Robert caught the sideways glance the ER nurse shot him. He took one last drag before he flicked his cigarette toward the street. It landed in the snow with a hiss. He certainly wasn't the *only* doctor there who smoked, but he was one of the very few who did. He knew it wasn't a good look, but he'd only just picked up the habit again. He checked his watch. The nurse was part of the shift change. He could leave now if he wanted to, but he was in no hurry to return home. Solitude made everything seem larger. Bare footsteps echoing off the hardwood floor of their dining room that, though it only sat eight, loomed like the feasting hall of some great castle. The endless California King with no edges, always waking in the middle no matter how many times he rolled. The kitchen table stretching on to infinity, nothing interrupting its polished oak surface, save the divorce papers that arrived just days ago.

Papers she had already signed.

The snow that sat atop his tight gray-flecked curls melted and ran in rivulets, cooling his scalp in dots. He cracked the knuckle of his ring finger. Slid the wedding band on and off, the light brown of his skin almost white underneath. An old habit, never used to the jewelry—any jewelry—but especially on his hands.

He was heading inside to get his keys when he heard the keening of a siren in the distance. He waited. The Doppler effect faded as the ambulance neared. It slid slightly before coming to a full stop under the archway. The siren shut off, but a muffled wail from inside the vehicle replaced it. The back doors swung open and a paramedic jumped down and helped his partner guide the gurney. A lanky young brother lay strapped down, tan hoodie soaked with blood. The sheet was crumpled at his feet from the writhing of his legs, and covered in urine and feces. His oxygen mask fogged with every moan.

Robert followed the paramedics inside and they briefed him on the way to the trauma unit. The bones of the left side of the kid's face had been crushed, and the right side was lined with fractures, likely from a secondary impact. Few teeth remained intact, and the bite from the impact had lacerated his tongue almost to the middle. Some of the shards from his orbital bone damaged the eye. He'd likely lose sight in it, if not the eye altogether. What neurological testing they had been able to complete when he wasn't seizing suggested he had a bleed in his brain.

The pieces of red mortar Robert plucked from his skin suggested someone had struck him with a brick. Had they thrown it? Dropped it on him? The force of the impact seemed impossible for one person to inflict on another.

The team of residents moved quickly to stabilize him. After paging the neurosurgeon on-call, the team had the kid transferred to the ICU. Robert removed his mask and gown, crumbled them and tossed them towards the trash. It fell short of the mark. One of the

EMTs stood with his back to the nurses' station, elbows propped on the counter, running game on a young aide. He saw the missed shot and tilted his chin at Robert.

"What's that they say about day jobs?" he asked.

Robert gave a half-hearted smile and joined them at the station to review the boy's chart. "Homewood," he said to himself. They shared a hometown, though Robert hadn't been back in years. Not since before Mama got sick. Then Pops died. Then Mama followed him home. A wash of overwhelming loneliness surged, then, with a sharp breath out, ebbed. He pushed the chart away.

"Probably some kind of retaliation," the EMT said.

Robert looked up. "I'm sorry?"

The EMT turned and leaned his arms on the counter, standing over Robert. The bulge of his jacket partially obscured his identification badge, but Robert made out the first name "Scott".

"The kid," he said. "Probably got attacked as a retaliation. His gangbanger buddy was there when we showed up."

"That boy wasn't wearing colors," Robert said. "But his friend was, so that says it all, I guess."

Scott shifted on his elbows. "You said it yourself, the kid's from Homewood. Do the math."

"I'm from Homewood," Robert said. "So what you're saying is black plus Homewood equals gang member. Is my math right?"

Scott stood up from the counter and ran his fingers through his hair, his pale cheeks flushed. "That's not what I meant and you know it."

"Right," Robert said. He stood and went to walk away, then stopped. "Let me ask you something. How long did it take you to get there?"

"Excuse me?" Scott said.

"When the call came in, and you heard a young black man had

31

been assaulted, did you hurry? Or did you finish getting the number of some aide at another hospital?"

"Are you calling me a racist?"

"And when you picked that young man up, did you do everything within your power on that ride here to save him, or did you think, well, it's just another banger off the street?"

Robert saw in his periphery the aide Scott had been talking to trading uncomfortable glances with the nurse next to Robert. Scott leaned his hands on the counter, his face tight, save a slight curl at his lip.

"You can go fuck yourself, Doc. You don't know a thing about me."

"Yeah," Robert said. "Yeah, I think I do."

Scott pushed away, hands up in mock surrender, and headed for the sliding doors to the parking lot. He grabbed his partner along the way and they left without a look back. Robert dropped back into his chair. He felt eyes on him and looked to his left to see Lorraine, the charge nurse, with wide eyes. Then a smirk creased her brown cheeks.

"Okay, Dr. Winston," she said. "I see you."

Robert winced. "Too much?"

"Please. Not enough."

Robert returned as genuine a smile as he could fabricate. He held no regret for what he'd said, but regretted the necessity. He reached for the chart again and read his name.

"Marcus Anderson," he said.

Had the boy been someone his mama might have known? Had his grandfather watched the Steelers on Sunday's with Robert's father?

"Lorraine, page me with updates on him, will you?"

She nodded and walked off to join others on the staff gathered around the station and listened to the weather report on the radio. The

32

Nor'easter approached. Those with long commutes prepped empty treatment rooms for an overnight stay. They joked and laughed. They didn't exclude Robert, but they didn't include him, either. Not that he blamed them. He enjoyed these rotations with the teaching hospital. He often, but not always, arrived to a certain level of celebrated respect. One thing remained constant, however, no matter where he went, especially with the trauma teams—he hadn't earned the camaraderie they'd formed in the trenches, and so, he often found himself alone, tonight more so than most.

He finished his notes, grabbed his coat from the hook behind the nurses' station and headed back outside. A gust sent icy air slicing through his scrubs and the long johns beneath. Leaning against his spot against the outside wall, he fished another cigarette from the bent soft pack in his front coat pocket. Savoring the cold fresh air, he took a deep inhale, closed his eyes, and saw the dining room table again.

She hadn't waited for his response. There it was, signed on every page next to the multicolored plastic arrow labels, directing his pen to the empty space where his name should go. *Tamara Winston.*

The day the papers arrived, he'd almost called her, but the last time he'd done that had been a mistake. Things were said, things worse than the time before, the time she decided more time apart was what they needed. She just had to go to her sister's, her Goddamned sister, who never liked Robert to begin with, who he knew, just *knew* relished the chance to drive home the wedge that threatened to cleave them completely in two. Disgusted at the notion of her whispering in Tamara's ear as though delivering an incantation, he stubbed the cigarette out into the tread of his sneakers and went back inside. He walked up to Lorraine seated at her desk.

"Any place close by to get a drink?" Robert asked her.

"You don't listen to the weather, huh?"

"It's not that bad out yet," Robert said. "Just one for the road."

"I'd head home if I were you. Those roads are going to get bad fast."

"Driving in the snow is in my blood," he said. "You want to join me?"

Lorraine raised her left hand, palm facing her and wiggled her fingers. A diamond caught the overhead lights and glinted.

Robert brought his hands to his chest in a mea culpa. "No disrespect."

"None taken," she said, smiling. "Lou's is a couple of blocks that way," she pointed west. "It's the closest if you want a quick drink. Not sure if it's the most hospitable, but you can take your chances." Robert tilted his head, not understanding her meaning. Lorraine scrunched her mouth and looked up at him from under her brow and Robert understood. Wrong bar for his complexion.

"Good looking out," he said. "See you tomorrow."

Outside, the flakes fell heavier. Cars rolled by, their tires muffled by the snow-quilted street. Robert popped the collar of his coat and pulled a knit cap from the pocket. He walked in the direction of Lou's. A salt truck rumbled past and peppered the windshields and doors with crystallized chunks that left pockmarks in the pristine white.

Robert and Tamara had said things they didn't mean, or at least said things they meant, but that should have been kept to themselves. In the weeks following the miscarriage, Tamara systematically withdrew from Robert. She had this infectious wide-mouthed laugh, complete with head toss, but devoid of pretension, punctuated by snorts if she really found something funny. She'd laughed like that on the exam table when they'd had their first ultrasound. The sanitary paper underneath her sounded like applause as she wriggled with excitement when they heard the rapid-fire heartbeat.

But there were no laughs at the final ultrasound. Just the sound of their own breath, held first in anticipation, then in fear, finally let out in a simultaneous slow sigh. A physician's assistant delivered the news. Robert guessed the doctor could only be bothered with the happy occasions, and in a way, he understood why. As a medical student, he'd been forced by his instructors to deliver bad news to terminal patients, or to family members when they'd lost someone dear. He'd felt a sense of physical pain when he had done it, as he imagined his teachers and professors had before him. It seemed less a hazing and more a rite of passage. Strange how clear it had seemed at that moment, as the assistant wiped the gel from Tamara's belly and replaced the ultrasound wand—the sound like a weapon being holstered.

"Your body has completed the miscarriage," she'd said.

"Take as long as you need," she'd said.

After they'd been left alone, Tamara and Robert had heard muffled sounds of excitement through the wall. Tamara took Robert's hand as he helped her from the table and dressed in a quiet daze. No tears. No words. Robert had guided her through the filled waiting room, his hands on her shoulders as if to protect her from paparazzi. The way they all looked at her, trying to look like they weren't looking at her, glancing up from their pregnancy magazines, bridal magazines, and gossip rags, he knew they knew what had happened and she didn't deserve their eyes on her. Down the hall to the elevator she looked up at Robert, her eyes brimming.

"I'm hungry," she said. She scrunched up her mouth in a half smile. He smiled back.

"I could eat," he said.

They ate a late breakfast at a restaurant near the OB's office. They hadn't yet warmed from the winter chill and Tamara swam in Robert's oversized hooded sweatshirt. She stirred at her dippy eggs with her fork, mixing the yolks with the mountain of ketchup she piled on top of them.

"Are you trying to find them?" Robert asked.

"What?"

"The eggs that came with your ketchup. Because I don't see them." She tried to hold back a smile. "Don't smile," he said. "It's not funny. I'm not kidding, I think we got ripped off." Her lips got tighter as she fought harder. Their waitress refilled their coffees and Tamara sipped. Robert leaned on the table. "You see? See how she looked at us?" he asked. "I bet you the white folks in here get eggs with their ketchup." Tamara spit back into her cup and wiped her mouth. She gave a slight snort. Robert smiled.

"You're so crazy," she said.

Robert had shrugged and grinned. They'd get through this. They were tough. They knew how to laugh. He reached for Tamara's hand and she reached back, but then her brow knit and her eyes narrowed. She clutched at her stomach. Her smile disappeared. She shifted in her seat and her eyes went wet in an instant.

"Robert," she whispered.

She looked down and shook her head. When she looked up, tears spilled down her cheeks. Robert slid into her side of the booth. Red stained the crotch of her gray sweatpants like a broken ink pen. Robert took off his sweater and wrapped it around her waist, dropped money on the table and hurried her out of the restaurant. Even at fifteen weeks, she'd been told to expect cramping, spotting, perhaps even some bleeding. She hadn't been told how to expect to feel. She curled in the fetal position in the back seat and quietly wept the whole way home.

That night and every night that followed, Tamara had edged farther away from the center of their bed and shied from Robert's touch when he'd reach across the gap. She went to bed fully dressed and showered with the master bathroom door closed.

Despite Robert's protests, she'd returned to work in a week. Her meetings ran later. They ate microwave dinners or takeout in front of the television. She hardly spoke, at least not to Robert. She spent hours on the phone with her sister in San Diego while he called up medical journal articles on the web, pretended not to listen, and tried to figure out what he'd done wrong.

The fight started after his third consecutive eight-to-eight shift going into the weekend. She'd finally decided she needed more time away from work and stayed home. Robert slept at the hospital to give her the space he thought she wanted. When he returned home, the trash had three days' worth of frozen breakfast, lunch, and dinner packaging and smelled like overripe bananas. The sink was full of stemless wine glasses with dried rings on the bottom. In the bedroom, her clothes hung from the treadmill, shirts plastered to the floor, panties draped over the edge of the wicker hamper.

The toilet flushed and she appeared in the doorway, silhouetted by the overhead light behind her. She wore what had become her new uniform: a durag, white long-sleeved thermal, heather gray sweatpants and suede slippers. She gave a slight jump at the sight of him, then walked past and climbed under the comforter and turned her back to him. He sat on the edge of the bed.

"Have you been outside today?" he asked. "Or yesterday?"

"Where have you been?" she asked.

"I didn't want to smother you."

She pulled the comforter back and slowly sat up. She spoke softly. "Can we, maybe, not make this about *you*? Please?"

"I'm sorry. Honestly, that's not what I meant."

"What did you mean?"

"I lost it, too, Tam."

"*It*? Do you always have to be so clinical?"

"No." Robert looked at his hands. The cold weather had dried them, made them ashy. The repeated handwashing after patient care cracked his flesh, left red slivers in between the light brown skin of his knuckles. "I couldn't think in terms of 'him' or 'her,'" he said. "That was just too hard."

"It was a girl," Tamara said. "I…think she was a girl."

"A girl. Did she have a name?" Tamara shook her head. "I wonder who she would have looked like."

She managed a weak smile.

"I know at our age this was a risk. That this might have been it. But we can try again." He winked at her, hoping for a real smile. "Isn't that the fun part anyway?" Robert reached for her but again she shied away. Robert's hand recoiled. "What, Tam? What did I do? What am I doing wrong that you won't even let me touch you? Tell me and I'll stop."

"I'm sorry that I'm not dealing with this the way you'd like me to. I can't pretend that she was an 'it.' I don't have your gift for detachment. But let's pretend that I'm already feeling bad enough without you making me feel guilty about not wanting to fuck you."

"Whoa, wait a minute, *what*? Tam, that is not what I'm trying to do."

Tamara wiped away a tear from her cheek with the heel of her hand. "I didn't want this baby and you made me want her and now she's gone."

"I *made* you?"

"I told you I didn't want one, but you pushed and you pushed and you pushed. Your mama just had to have a grandbaby and you couldn't say no, could you? You couldn't let me say no."

"Okay. You're angry. We're going to say something stupid. You need some space."

"Stop telling me what I need, Robert. We didn't *need* this baby. We were doing fine, just you and me."

38

Weary of defending himself for days, he snapped.

"Well, I guess you showed me, didn't you?" he said.

He sighed the instant the words left his mouth, disgusted with himself, but it was too late. Tamara gave him an incredulous look and hugged herself. He knew he should have crossed to the other side and pulled her close but her accusation cut deep and scraped bone. They were both proud, sometimes to the point of absurdity, and in that moment the distance between them felt immeasurable.

Tamara wiped at her eyes and curled into herself under the comforter, her back to Robert. He kneeled on the mattress and reached for her. He was going to pull her in close, even if she fought. Let her yell at him, hit him, if that's what it took. Let loose that pain so they could get back to where they had been. The box springs creaked under his weight and Tamara spoke, almost too quiet to hear.

"I'd like to go to sleep now," she'd said.

The determination in her voice withered Robert's resolve. He stepped away from the bed and gently closed the bedroom door behind him.

He paused. The wood floor squeaked as Tamara got out of bed. Then he heard the gentle whir of the oscillating fan she kept on her side of the bed. She couldn't sleep without the white noise to lull her to sleep, the same way Robert always stuck his leg out from under the comforter. Neither of them understood the other's quirky sleep behavior, and they had laughed about how restless they were when they tried one night to go without indulging their strange habits.

She never could sleep without the fan.

He wondered if she could sleep without him.

The next morning, neither of them had talked about the fight. They didn't talk about anything. The argument hung in the air like radioactive fallout, made all the more potent by their refusal to acknowledge it. Before Robert had worked up the courage to offer to stay home from work, Tamara had already headed up the stairs and back to their bedroom.

When he returned home, Tamara sat at the kitchen table, her eyes red-rimmed. Her hair was done, and she'd changed out of her sweats into a blouse and jeans. Robert sat across from her. She looked into his eyes.

"I'm leaving for a while," she said.

"No, you're not."

"I have to," she said. "Just for a while."

"Tamara, I'm so sorry."

"I know you are," she said. "I am, too. But the fact that we said those things, Robert, something's wrong. With us."

"We lost a child, Tam."

"I think maybe we lost a little of ourselves, too, Robert, and I need some time to figure out if that's the case. I can't do that here."

Robert clasped his hands and brought them to his mouth. He wanted to argue and make her stay, but he'd felt it, too, this river across which the two of them stood on opposite sides, neither of them with the means to ford it.

"What if I say no?"

"This isn't your decision," she said.

"Where will you go?"

"My sister's."

"California?" Robert said. He blew out. "Well, can I drive you to the airport?"

"The shuttle is already on its way."

Minutes later, Robert loaded Tamara's suitcases into the back of the idling shuttle van.

"You packed a lot," he said.

She put her hand on his cheek and he inhaled. The cocoa butter that softened her skin made her smell like home and he swallowed hard against the knot forming in his throat. He kissed her palm and promised to call. She didn't return the promise. The shuttle drove away, the taillights lighting the flakes that had just begun to fall.

A little more than a year had done nothing to dull the edges. Robert reached Lou's. The red neon sign buzzed above the entrance to the bar. Robert stomped the snow from his shoes and went inside. Just one drink. A warm up, for perhaps the beginning of a new tradition. To remember, by forgetting.

CHAPTER FOUR

Nico smiled at Isabel when she walked in to Lou's. She hoped he was feeling generous.

Only hours ago, eight white drunken college kids in burlap pullovers and Birkenstocks with thick wool socks had strolled into the diner. Rich kids dressing like they were poor. Refill after refill, food added on when one friend, then another, showed up late, milkshakes all around, and western omelets sent back already half-eaten because they were too cold. But with every belligerent order, every juvenile command, she smiled, always smiled, and each time she walked away they laughed at her. At the stains on her uniform, too tight around her stomach. Her too-high hair, her too-bright lipstick. They pretended to whisper, but she could tell they wanted her to hear. She did. But halfway through the month, she and Bobby were still short on rent, and their need for shelter took priority over pride. Sometimes all too often.

She almost never added on the tip for large parties. She preferred to earn it, and she *had* from this bunch. An unforgiving landlord, however, dictated a little insurance. She added up the large bill, dancing from foot to foot. She had needed to pee for the last hour. She dropped the check and headed to the bathroom. Elbows on her knees, she let out a whoosh of relief. Maybe they wouldn't notice the added gratuity and tip on top of that. The snow had started late enough not to affect her shift and it had been a good night. Thirty percent or more on that table would be a nice little take-home. Maybe even enough to take a day off, maybe convince Bobby to go catch a late-run flick at the cheap seats, like she used to do with him when he was little. She'd been cutting back on the booze for almost two weeks and as a result, they'd been talking more, in the rare moments when neither of them was working. Last week, he'd lifted his nose from his comics to ask her how her day was.

He'd even smiled.

When she returned from the bathroom, the kids were gone. The table was carnage. Full sugar packets stuffed into half-full coffee cups, soaked brown and swollen. A glass knocked over, water on the floor collecting from a thin stream above. In the puddle on the table sat the check, unpaid, the ink blurred, but just readable enough to see the words "Fuck You" scrawled across it. Isabel stared at it, then pulled it from the table, letting it drip before she squashed it in her fist and threw it with a wet slap against the floor. Patrons at a few lingering tables cast sideways glances at her.

"Fuck you, too," Isabel whispered to herself. She cleaned up her station and walked to the front to close out for the night.

Pockets, the manager, cashed out another waitress while Isabel waited her turn. She knew the policy on dine-and-dashers, but she hoped Pockets could see past to let her slide on this one. He had been in recovery, though for a lot longer and more consistently than she.

On slower nights, he'd talked to her, swapped horror stories of ruined relationships, both familial and otherwise. He often tried to convince her to come to a meeting, even offered to be her sponsor. Isabel never saw herself sitting amongst strangers and giving confession. Still, she'd considered, but didn't entirely trust his motivation. He was many years her senior, but kindly, more fatherly, with gin blossoms spread across his nose and the puffy cheeks that gave him his nickname. Though he never said anything inappropriate, she'd catch his stares from time to time. Watched his face bloom red when she covered her chest after seeing him look down her cleavage while counting out her tip shares at the end of a shift. With every invitation to join him at a meeting, she'd politely decline, but felt guilt for the disappointed smile he'd give her.

When it was her turn, she slid over her cash and checks, and pulled the scrunchie from her ponytail. Her curly black hair fell to the middle of her back and she swept the length over her shoulder. Pockets plunked at the adding machine keys and frowned.

"You're short," he said.

"And you're chubby." She gave him two finger pistols and winked.

"Very funny. But seriously. You're way off."

"That last table ditched, Pockets."

"What? How?"

"I had to pee. I came right back. You didn't see them leave?"

"Jesus, Izzy. That's an eighty-dollar check."

"I know, I know. Can't you just write it off or something?"

"You know I can't do that."

"It's over half my tips, Pockets."

"I hear you, Izzy. But your station is your responsibility, and if I let you slide…"

"Yeah, yeah, yeah, you have to do it for everyone. I'm not a fucking child, Pockets. Don't lecture me like one." Easing up on drinking made her *more* emotional, not less, the headaches more frequent and persistent. She knew Pockets had to answer to the owners, had his own job to worry about. "Sorry," she said. "It's fine. Whatever." She counted out the amount in fives and ones and laughed at the pathetic amount in her hand, just a little more than the bank she'd brought to make change for the night.

Pockets recounted, facing the bills all in the same direction. "I could probably give you a double tomorrow, if the snow doesn't shut us down. Interested?"

Isabel nodded yes, but to what, she didn't know. She wasn't listening. She remembered which nights Nico was on the bar at Lou's.

Her face numb from the chill outside, the familiar humid air smelled of beer and old fryer grease and warmed her cheeks when she opened the door. She winked at Nico and he returned the gesture.

Thank God, he seemed to be in a good mood.

The bar was mostly empty. All but the regulars had cleared out. Even on a weeknight, Lou's had a decent crowd. It was just enough of a dive to be cool for the college kids, but tonight, the electronic dartboard was quiet. No pool balls clacked, no frat boys hovered around the MegaTouch to play the match game with the soft-core porno pictures. Just the few sad sacks who'd been there since the place opened, hunched over their beers in the unsteady glow of the television above the bar. Nico went on about something, pointing at the screen showing highlights of the O.J. trial on Sports Center. Isabel pulled up a stool to join her people and they gave her a head nod and a friendly grumble.

"Its bullshit is all I'm saying," Nico said. "That cop's a witness, he ain't on trial."

"That's right," said an old-timer with a loose neck. "On the force twenty-five years, didn't none of these jagoff lawyers ever question me like they're doing this Fuhrman fella." More grumbles of support from the other regulars. Their heads bobbed like pigeons in agreement.

"Damn straight," Nico said. "Who gives a shit if he said nigger or not?"

"Easy, Nico," Isabel said. "Simmer."

"Hey, I'm saying it's a bad look, making the cop seem like the bad guy. They got it rough enough after that Rodney King nonsense. Suddenly all police are boogeymen because they beat down a junkie? Come off it."

"Exactly," the old-timer said. "My boy is on the force now, and he's wearing a vest on his beat. These gang punks are shooting at cops."

"It's shameful," Nico said. "The only reason they can even get away with it is because O.J.'s got enough dough for his Super Jew lawyer. Everyone knows he fucking did it."

"You know, fellas," Isabel said, "the only way Nico can see over that bar is when he's standing on his soapbox like that." The barflies chuckled and Nico mugged at her.

"See, boys," he said. "This type of common sense discussion is lost on Miss ACLU here." Isabel smirked and gave him the finger. "How'd you make out tonight, beautiful?" he asked, laughing.

Isabel's smiled faded. Her eyes stung and her cheeks went hot as she shook her head. Nico's shoulders dropped.

"What happened?"

"Buy a girl a drink?"

"My soapbox isn't tall enough to reach the vodka. Besides, ain't you supposed to be on the wagon? What's it been? A day?"

Isabel knew he was only trying to make her laugh, but her head throbbed, worse than before. She shouldn't be here. She'd promised Bobby. I can do anything for a month, she'd said. Yet here she was. Just one, she thought. She knew that one drink would lead to another, that she'd spend money they didn't have, and where would that get her? Get *them*? Yes, she could pick up more shifts, and so could Bobby. They'd come close to missing rent before and they'd always made it, though more often than not, Bobby did the heavy lifting. Good looking kid, better restaurant, better tips. But each time he picked up another shift, each time he gave up a precious day off, he got that look. That well-rehearsed, resigned disappointment that broke Isabel's heart more and more each time, that made her make the same empty promises to herself that this was the last time she'd ask him to do that. The idea of seeing that look again tonight made her anxious. Being anxious made her want to drink again, and wanting to drink again made her angry. She pushed away from the bar and stood to leave.

"Hey, where you going?" Nico asked. "Come on, I'm messing. Sit down."

She paused.

Just one.

She sat.

"It wasn't even my fault this time, Nico. I swear."

"Fucking Pockets," he said. "Probably would have let you off the hook if you'd a thrown him a mercy bang."

"Don't be gross." Nico reached to the shelf behind him and grabbed a bottle of Absolut. "You know I can't afford that," Isabel said. "Especially not now."

"Shut up." He smiled and topped the filled Collin's glass with a splash of tonic. She took a long sip from the straw and felt the panic fade. How she missed that taste, the effervescence of the carbonation on her tongue, the tingle on the inside of her cheeks. No kerosene in this glass, not like the cheap shit that used to sit in a plastic bottle in the freezer at home. A nice, smooth burn with just enough sweet from the tonic. "So what, he suspended you again?"

She closed her eyes and took another long pull on the straw and emptied the glass. The stuttered sucking sound surprised her and she opened her eyes to see Nico, his arms folded and smirking.

"Jesus, you got canned?"

Her face went flush again. She hadn't eaten much and the vodka settled home quickly. "No," she said, pouty. "But I might as well have. Got dine-and-dashed."

"Ah, shit," he said. "And you had to eat it?"

She nodded. "He did offer me a split shift tomorrow, so I might make some of it back. Except for this freaking snow."

Nico refilled her drink but she waved her hands in protest. "Stop," he said. "On the house tonight."

Isabel raised her glass to him and took a smaller sip.

Finish this one slow and go home. Back on the wagon tomorrow.

It was difficult, though, slowing down. Nico made a damn fine drink and it took all she had not to suck this one down, too.

"Nursing it, huh?" he asked.

"I don't and you'll need to drive me home."

"That's what I was hoping."

Nico was cute in his way, a bit of a mook, but a good Sicilian boy. He was definitely too short and kind of doughy around the middle. He wore his shirts too tight, but he had nice arms. His jokes were corny, and the cologne was always a bit much, but he had a swagger that Isabel found adorable and he made her laugh. But he liked her too much. She wanted to keep it casual, and he'd said the "m" word more than once in the sweaty warmth of a post-romp glow. Not to mention he wasn't very good about keeping her from her predilections. Bobby knew it, too, and didn't like her spending time with Nico, so the nights he convinced her to spend with him were almost always at his place. She knew all the reasons Nico was wrong for her, but he was comfortable. Safe, though not really. She needed to finish her drink and go.

Isabel took short sips and let the ice water down her drink while Nico and his cronies went on about the trial, how all the politically correct bullshit after the L.A. riots made it so he was going to get away with it all, and how "Slick Willy" Clinton was going to put every one of them in the poor house. Isabel rolled her eyes. Had she missed how full of shit they all were because she had been too drunk to notice? She took her last diluted sip and pushed the glass away. Nico went to refill it and she placed a cocktail napkin on top.

"I'm good," she said.

"Come on. I'm going to give last call soon on account of this snow. One more and walk out with me."

Isabel knew that look. It had been a while and considering the night she had, Nico lying next to her didn't sound so bad. She dreaded the thought of another conversation about why she didn't want to settle down, but she didn't want to go home and face Bobby's disappointment. She'd stay the night with Nico and get that double to make up for the lost cash. She smiled at him but kept her hand over the glass.

"Hurry up," she said.

Nico cleaned his draft glasses with renewed vigor when the front door opened and sucked in cold air. A tall black man brushed snow from his shoulders and sat a few stools down from Isabel. The regulars stopped their conversations short and stared into their beers.

"Already gave last call, bro," Nico said.

Isabel hated when Nico did that; the condescending pseudo-street talk anytime a black man came into the bar. She shot him a hard look. Nico scrunched up his mouth at her, then held up his index finger to the man to indicate he'd allow for one drink. The man caught the gesture from Isabel and lifted his chin towards her.

"Thanks for that," he said.

Isabel jerked her chin back at him.

That voice. How did she know that voice?

Nico poured his drink and Isabel stared and tried not to look like she was staring. He gave her a second, then a third glance, with a look like he knew he knew her, but he couldn't figure out how. Embarrassed to be caught watching, Isabel tipped back her nearly empty glass. The ice that stuck to the bottom smacked off her teeth and water ran down her chin. Nico offered her a cocktail napkin and she snatched it. She did her best to wipe her face, tried not to look like another sloppy drunk, and wondered why she all of a sudden gave a damn what this guy thought.

"Buy you one more for last call?" the man asked. "Since you got him to give me one."

The voice registered this time, and adrenaline dumped into Isabel's bloodstream. The smells of fried bar food suddenly overpowering and repugnant. The ice cubes in her glass split as they melted, like the crack before an avalanche. She turned the glass in circles in the pool of water at the bottom of it and ran her thumbs up and down the sweating edges. The man watched her. Nico watched her. Everyone goddamn watched her. Her throat felt swollen and incapable of speech. She nodded at the man with a tight smile. The man cocked his head at her non-answer and Nico intervened.

"She's good," Nico said. "Fifteen minutes and we're closing up."

The man sipped his scotch, bared his teeth and let out a hiss. God, it *was* him. Old habits died hard. Anger built. This was *her* bar. *Her* spot. What was he doing here? She wanted to hate him just because she remembered the way he always did that when he drank scotch. To hate him for the fact that it was still endearing, because who drank scotch as a college student? She wanted to hate him for still being so goddamn handsome, for the fact that more than two decades had done little to age him.

A little softer around the jaw, maybe, the hairline back a little further. Still a stunner. Yet for all that hate she tried to drum up, she felt something else. Something other than anger that she didn't still know existed for him, something she told herself she'd never feel for him again. Yet here he was and she realized that all those self-reassurances had been bullshit.

Then she laughed. Just a little bark to herself. No time for dinner coupled with Nico's heavy pours left her a little buzzed.

No way it's him.

"Something funny?" he asked.

"Huh?" she said.

"I thought you laughed?"

She shook her head, tight lipped. If it wasn't him, why couldn't she talk? Why could she barely look at him? Nico hovered between two of them, incessantly polishing the same draft glass. His eyes ricocheted back and forth between the two of them.

"Well, anyway, thanks again," he said to Isabel. "I needed that." He reached into his back pocket and pointing at her empty glass. "That one's on me."

He closed his eyes and cursed under his breath as his hand came back from his pocket empty.

"Come on, bro," Nico said.

"I swear to God," he said, "it's back in my locker at the hospital. I'm a doctor. I've got cash and credit. It'll take me ten minutes to walk over and get it, tops."

"And ten to walk back," Nico said. He gestured towards Isabel. "We're trying to get out of here before this storm gets out of hand." Isabel gave Nico another dirty look. He returned a confused one.

The man searched the counter and then pulled a matchbook from a draft glass full of them on the bar. He scrawled something on it and handed it to Nico.

"I'll be back tomorrow night with double what I owe," the man said. "Call me at this number if I'm not. I'm really sorry."

"Yeah, I'll hold my breath," Nico said.

The man apologized to them both again and walked out the door. When he was gone, Nico looked down at the matchbook and laughed.

"Doctor, my ass," he said. "Probably some fucking orderly. And what's with you, anyway? You know him or something? You looked like you were going to puke."

Isabel's throat unclenched. "I saw a ghost."

"You mean a spook," Nico said. The barflies laughed. Nico slung his dishrag over his shoulder and affectionately berated them to go home. He tossed the matchbook on the bar. Isabel stood and slunk her way down the bar to read it. Nico's wet fingers streaked the ink, but the name was clear.

Robert Winston.

Bobby's father.

Isabel braced herself on the bar. Her pulse thrummed in her ears and her skin felt pinpricked. She bolted for the door. Outside, she looked up and down the street, looking for the phantom memory of a man who'd come and gone like he'd done so well in the past. She saw a silhouette of a figure through a curtain of snowflakes, then take the corner and disappear. She put her hands on her knees and dry-heaved. Nico ran up behind her and grasped her shoulders.

"You all right?" he asked.

"Uh-huh," she said. She forced a smile. "Guess I turned into a lightweight." Nico guided her back to the door but she pulled away and patted his cheek. "I'm going to call it a night, okay? I'll call you?"

"What? You sure?"

"I'm good, hon."

"Yeah, okay," Nico said. He put his hands in his pockets and went back inside.

Isabel pulled into a space in front of the apartment. The bare tires slid in the snow and the right front one went up on the curb. She opened her door, then stopped, pulling it shut again. The snow fell heavier, her windshield a television gone off the air until morning. She chewed at the inside of her cheek. No way to explain this to Bobby to make him understand.

The lost money, the vodka on her breath. His father, supposed to be dead all these years, at a bar she said she'd stay away from. Her hands gripped the steering wheel. She tasted blood from the ruined skin in her cheek and tongued the wound.

No light through the window of their basement apartment. Still at work or asleep. Either way, a temporary reprieve.

The hallway held no more warmth than outside. Isabel stomped snow out of her waffle-soled shoes and water soaked into the filthy carpeting. A Columbo rerun blasted at full volume from the next apartment. As she unlocked the door, her keys jangled from the collection of novelty key chains with her name on them. Cartoon characters whose decorative paint had worn away. Childhood gifts from Bobby. Though they bulged in her pocket, she had never once thought of throwing them away.

Isabel gently shouldered the door open, taking care not to let it catch on the shag carpeting. She whispered for Bobby while her eyes adjusted to the dark.

Silence. No breathing, no snoring.

A car's headlights swept through the window. Bobby's sheet and blanket sat folded in a perfect square atop his pillow on the couch. She breathed out and walked her hands along the wall through the dark hallway to her bedroom. She turned on the light, tossed her keys on the dresser with a clunk and fell backwards onto her mattress. The bare light bulb faintly buzzed. She stared at the water stains on the ceiling. Nights Bobby couldn't sleep they'd lay together and pretend they were different continents, fantasy lands from his books, except there *they'd* rule as queen and prince, kind but not to be trifled with. She'd ask him to list the names of his dragons and all the warriors in their armies until he'd drift back to sleep.

She repeated the names she remembered to herself and her eyelids weighed heavy, exhausted by the emotion of the last few hours. She blinked them open and sat up. She'd rushed home not just to beat Bobby there, but because of something she wanted to see in secret.

Over in the closet, she retrieved a box of photos from the back shelf. She rifled through Polaroids and photo booth strips, senior portraits, baby pictures, and family shots.

Where was it? Had she gotten rid of it?

She tossed them all to the side, then stopped. She found one she wasn't looking for but couldn't help but look at again.

Bobby's kindergarten graduation. He was so handsome. They had these adorable caps and gowns. Little men and women with fingers up their noses dancing like they had to pee. Not Bobby. His beautiful black hair stuck out from the sides of his cap like wings. Isabel told him once that she couldn't let him outside in the wind or he would take off and fly away and leave her all alone. Then she whooshed him up into the air and he giggled that little laugh and stuck out his arms like a plane. He had the tiniest little gaps between his Chiclet-sized teeth, almost too big for his mouth, his smile so perfect in its imperfection. Things were much simpler then, if only for a time. He had smiled so much more. They both did. She set that photo aside and kept looking. Then she found it at the bottom of the pile.

Robert and Isabel. One of the park employees at Kennywood had taken it for them during the only real date they'd had. The exit for the Steel Phantom stood in the background. They had just left the coaster and her hair was a mess. Robert had whispered something in her ear just as the camera flashed and caught her, mouth wide open and laughing.

Stop it. Don't you romanticize this again.

Isabel held Bobby's graduation picture next to the photo of her and Robert so that their faces were right next to each other.

God, so alike, but so different.

Could she do it? Put aside her anger?

Maybe Bobby would smile again, a real one, big and bright, cheeks pushing his eyes into slits. Her little boy, not hardened and bitter by the world he lived in now, the one he had no hand in creating. He deserved a chance to have his father in his life. But what did that mean? For her? For Bobby? The idea of her son protected and happy had more weight and warmth, but there was no guarantee that would be the outcome.

It didn't seem so scary when she looked at that kindergarten smile, even though it meant she could lose everything.

She set the two pictures on the nightstand and walked back to her closet with the box of the rest. She pushed it back on the shelf, up against the wall when her hand brushed a bottle. A "break in case of emergency" stash she stowed away after she swore to Bobby to give sobriety an honest go.

"You promised," she said out loud.

She turned to leave the closet, but one hand lingered on the shelf, as if pulled by an incensed child insisting they be allowed to play just five more minutes.

She pulled down the bottle and took three long slugs. Tomorrow would be a big day, after all, and she needed to get some sleep. She hoped Bobby was safe with all this snow.

CHAPTER FIVE

A truck chirped in reverse as its plow scraped the asphalt. The sound woke Bobby. Dried drool had glued fibers of the carpet to his face. He pushed himself up and peeked over the edge of the bed. Aaron hadn't moved. The room had black shades and he had no idea of the time. Maybe he hadn't been asleep that long. The plows meant the streets might have been cleared, which meant the buses might be running.

The door hinges squeaked as he pulled it open, just wide enough to squeeze through and the floor cracked and groaned. Why was everything so loud when he didn't want to be heard? He looked back but Aaron didn't move. He snuck down the hall past Cort, dead asleep on the couch with his hand down his pants.

It was bright outside, but Bobby couldn't see the sun. Wispy gray clouds turned black as they passed in front of it, like smoke from a building fire. The plows hadn't made it to the side streets. They never seemed to have time for the shitty neighborhoods, even though that's where the people who needed to get to work the most lived.

Bobby tucked his pants into his boots and hiked through the shin-high snow. Every few steps, he turned to look over his shoulder. Each time he expected to see Aaron behind him.

What am I so afraid of? Jesus. He said he'd never hurt me.

No, wait. He'd asked if I thought he'd ever hurt me. He never said he wouldn't.

Bobby'd lied to him for as long as he'd known him. Something in Aaron's voice last night when he told Bobby about the meaning of his last name—the crooked smiles—seemed to say that he knew and didn't know all at once. Bobby heard Aaron's voice in his head again about animals that needed to be put down.

All too familiar, though never before from Aaron.

Bobby found a sheltered bus stop on Fifth Avenue. Car tires sizzled along the wet road. He sat on the bench and leaned his head against the Plexiglas. The scratched plastic reminded him of the window separating him and Aaron in prison. He pulled his head away.

He used to get night terrors as a kid. His bed would be soaked with piss and sweat, and Isabel would come in to hold him. He didn't mind the booze on her breath as much then, since it made it so he couldn't smell his own pee. She'd say, don't worry, the terrors are only scary at night. In the light of day, you'll see how silly they are. Things are always scarier at nighttime. She'd lift his chin, smiling. *That's why they're not called day terrors.*

He'd fall back asleep knowing morning was coming and the terrors wouldn't hurt him. But there in the bus shelter, he sat terrified. Terrified of the guy who used to be his best friend, terrified about what he had done, terrified about what he might do, about what he'd become.

Terrified that, in more ways than one, he might have had a hand in that.

The bus hit a pothole. The hotels and studio apartments of Oakland and Shadyside gave way to rowhomes and bars, like the descending half of a bell curve that reminded Bobby that his normal was not in the middle. The bus rumbled over thick bumps of packed snow down Frankstown Avenue. Bobby pulled the cord. When he rounded the corner, he saw the passenger-side tire of the Fox up on the curb.

Isabel was home.

For the first time in as long as he could remember, Bobby felt relieved she was.

The Price is Right blasted from behind the door of their neighbor's apartment. They never actually saw anyone come or go, and every time Bobby walked past that door, the smell of cat piss was stronger than that of the mildew embedded in the hall carpet. He wondered sometimes if someone was dead in there and if so, what the police would do with the television. The sound only stopped when stations went off the air. The white noise helped Bobby sleep. As Bobby unlocked his door, somebody bid a dollar and won a new jet ski.

Bobby shoved the door away from the warped jamb and called into the apartment for Isabel. No answer. Then snoring. He pulled a mason jar from the cabinet above the sink to add his tips to hers, but when he counted it out, it was little more than the night before. *Had she not gone to work?* Two weeks until rent was due. He would need to pick up another double. She would, too. He made his way to her bedroom. Next door somebody guessed the actual retail price and won a thousand dollars and a china cabinet.

The door was open a crack. Static-filled jazz filtered from the clock radio on the nightstand. He slowly pushed it open and peered in. Isabel lay on her back, open-mouthed while her guttural snores reverberated in the tiny room. Bobby had heard those snores before, though not for weeks. Two to be exact. He followed her arm as it hung from the edge of the bed, her fingers draped across the top of a plastic handle of Popov's Vodka. Empty.

"You've got to be fucking kidding me," he whispered.

A snore caught in her throat and she coughed and stirred but rolled to her side and stayed asleep. For a moment, Bobby's anger superseded his fear. Things had been going so much better, yet she hadn't been able to make it a month. Every time, when he needed her the most, she had shown him that he couldn't rely on her at all. He'd have to handle this situation with Aaron himself, although God knew how he'd do that. But he had to know why she'd slipped again.

He threw the door open so hard it slammed off the wall. She sat up with a start and grabbed her head. Bobby leaned in the doorway, arms folded, and waited for her webs to clear. She groaned and pressed the heel of her palm into her forehead. She blinked away the brightness of the room and swung her feet to the floor, knocking over the empty bottle.

"Shit," she said, softly.

"Tell me about it," he said.

"Go ahead," she said. "Let me have it. I deserve it."

Bobby watched her from the doorway, silent. She looked over at him from beneath her mess of curls. "Go on," she said.

"We have two weeks," he said, quietly. "And the jar might as well be empty."

"I had it, Bobby. I was almost all the way there."

"And?"

"Does it matter? You've already made up your mind that I screwed up."

"Did you?"

She put her head in her hands and groaned. "Yes and no."

On the other side of the wall, somebody lost a game of Plinko and the losing horns sounded. Bobby laughed at the timing of the sound in spite of himself. So did Isabel. It felt good, like a steam pipe vented of pressure. He uncrossed his arms and sat next to Isabel on the bed. He rolled the overturned vodka bottle under his foot.

"You promised," he said. Isabel dragged her fingers under her eyes to wipe at tears before they fell.

"I know I did," she said.

"This where the rent went?"

She appeared insulted by the question and turned to Bobby with anger in her eyes, but the lines in her face softened when she looked at him. She tucked a stray hair behind his ear. The gel had worn off and his hair slowly retracted into their natural curls. He could see that she had something to tell him, but he couldn't tell what. Her mouth scrunched and a tear spilled down her face.

"No," she said. "That's not where it went."

Bobby wanted to push for more, but then she might have had questions of her own, namely why he had just gotten home. He hadn't thought of that in his immediate anger, let alone what his story would be. She stared at her feet and he didn't press her further.

"Think you can pick up a double?" she asked.

Bobby nodded. "Can you?"

"Sure," she said.

Bobby's grandfather loved poker. He took Bobby to a game once with a bunch of his retired cop friends. He told him to watch the other players for fidgeting. The way they played with their chips. Which direction their eyes went after they looked at their cards. He said everyone had a tell. Little tics, even things they said and how they said it made them for a liar. It didn't take Bobby long to figure out that Isabel had a tell, too.

It was "sure."

She might have been able to pick up a double, but she wasn't *going* to. It was in her voice. Of that, *he* was sure. He shook his head and went to leave. Isabel called out after him.

"Where were you, anyway?"

Fuck.

"What?"

"You just got home, right?"

"Aaron's back," Bobby said.

"From prison?"

"Yep."

"I should have let you have the car," she said. "Did you know he was getting out?"

"Nope. It's fine."

He leaned on the jamb again and picked at callouses where his palm met his fingers, thickened from years of stacking milk crates and carrying hot dinner plates. He uncovered the new pink skin underneath, then rolled the dead skin into little pills and let them drop to the floor. He wanted Isabel to hold him. Make the day go away. Stop drinking and not break promises. Don't ask him to work even more. Protect him the way she's supposed to. Don't lie to him the way she seemed to feel she had to. He stared at the skin where the callouses had been. If it were only that easy, to peel everything off and start over. His eyes stung and his nose ran.

"Did something happen?" she asked.

Bobby turned his back to her as he wiped at his eyes. "You can have the car again tonight," he said. "I just have to get a shower and get changed."

"Wait." She came up behind him. "I know this looks like I messed up really bad, but I *promise* there's a reason. For the money, for the vodka, all of it. I just need to work something out first and I swear to you it will all make sense. I will make this right, okay?"

"Yeah, okay." His voice wavered. Isabel placed a hand on his shoulder.

"Do you trust me?" she asked.

"Sure," he said, and closed the door behind him.

CHAPTER
SIX

Bobby made it to the bistro in time to send one of the lunch crew home, but the rush was shit. Nothing but tables of office park employees who only wanted appetizers and camped out in his station with refill after refill of coffee. He stared at the computer screen and tried to remember what the lady at table thirty-five had ordered for dessert. Normally he could easily memorize a ten-top's order without writing it down, but today he couldn't recall what she wanted. *Who ordered dessert at three in the afternoon anyway?*

Twelve hours of fear had worn him down. The vapid customer idiosyncrasies that tended to merely annoy him now made him feel borderline homicidal. He'd seen other servers dish revenge with a squirt of Visine into a rude guest's coffee or watched them spit on the underside of their burger bun and then sit back and watch the show. He'd been tempted on more than one occasion to follow suit, though he never had. Now he wanted to go back to the dining room and wrap his hands around that woman's neck. He surprised himself with his hostility, when hours ago he was faced with true viciousness, real violence with real consequences yet to be meted. Still, in some ways, it felt kind of good to feel something other than afraid. But the feeling was fleeting.

Aaron walked into the kitchen. He wore his back-of-the-house checkered pants tucked into his boots and had a white long-sleeved line cook's jacket slung over his shoulder. He stopped short when he saw Bobby at the computer.

"Hey," he said. "There you are. Where did you go?"

Russell yelled out from the hot food window where he pulled down plates to garnish them with sauces. "Cover them up, Aaron." He pointed at the tattoos on Aaron's arms. Aaron rolled his eyes and put on his jacket.

"What are you doing here?" Bobby asked. Aaron had never needed to work, but the restaurant had been a great front for his dealing weed before he got caught. He cleared more money in a night than Bobby did in a week of closing shifts. "Back in business?" Bobby asked.

"Condition of my parole," he said. "I don't have to wear an ankle bracelet as long as I check in and Russell vouches for me. We set it up before I got out. I made him promise not to tell you I was coming back so I could surprise you last night."

Bobby nodded. He'd definitely done that. He went back to his computer screen, but Aaron didn't leave. His voice lowered. "So seriously, where did you go?"

Bobby looked up. Aaron's face had changed. Though he couldn't be sure, Bobby thought he saw worry there. Maybe even fear. Had the consequences of what he'd done finally registered?

Aaron's eyes traced Bobby's face. He assessed him, scanned him like some kind of cyborg, wondering if Bobby had told Isabel, the police, anyone he shouldn't have. Bobby felt that lightness in his feet again, the sense that his body was not his own and he wondered how young was too young for a stroke. Aaron waited for his answer as the shift change filtered into the kitchen. One of the servers Bobby knew had a closing shift walked behind Aaron. Bobby stepped around Aaron and tugged on the server's shirt as he passed.

"Hey, you want the night off?" Bobby asked.

The server looked much the worse for wear. "Fuck yes," he said, running his hand through his hair. "I think I'm still drunk. Shit, I have a follow, though."

"No sweat. I got it," Bobby said.

A follow meant Bobby made minimum wage on top of tips while a trainee more or less did the work for him. He and Isabel might make the rent if he didn't end up in jail or dead. The server walked over to Russell at the food window to let him know about the switch. Bobby turned back to a waiting and increasingly impatient Aaron.

"So?" Aaron asked.

Russell called out again. "Bobby, run this broccoli cheese soup to ninety-five, will you?"

"You want to take your tie out of it first?" Bobby asked.

Russell looked down, unclipped his tie and threw it to the counter with a wet slap before he dished up a new cup. A prep cook slid the cheesecake Bobby had ordered through the window. Aaron watched him while he grabbed them both to run them out to the dining room. Bobby looked back. Aaron was still staring.

"Got to run these," Bobby said. He held the plates in front of his face and hustled out. He heard Aaron suck his teeth as he walked towards the back of the kitchen.

Bobby dropped off the food and leaned against the bus stand in his station. He came up with as many reasons as he could to tell Aaron why he had left before he woke up.

That he might have killed someone and that he was an accessory for driving off? That was a good reason.

That he'd hidden the fact that he had a black father for all the years they'd known each other and that he thought he'd hurt him even worse than that kid at the "O" if he found out? That was another good one.

Bobby pushed the heels of his hands into his eyes until they squished, and fireworks went off behind his lids. He had no idea what to do and the fear and uncertainty smothered him.

Shift change meant shift meeting at the back of the restaurant. More of the servers smoked than didn't, and after some bitching from those who didn't, everyone bundled up to meet on the back dock. They shifted from foot to foot to stay warm, their smoke mixing with the steam from their breath. Michelle, Bobby's now-trainee for the night, stood next to him. She wore black stretch pants and boots with the laces undone. Hair dyed blood-red poked out from under her longshoreman's cap. Bobby rolled his eyes as Russell prattled on about servers not ringing in desserts and employee theft. While some servers drifted off, others had side conversations about which ethnicity busboy was behind the thefts. Bobby had his suspicions. He eyed Luis, who interpreted the stare and flashed him the finger. Michelle scribbled down every word Russell said like a reporter, and her enthusiasm irritated Bobby instantly.

Aaron stood next to Russell. Bobby stared, not meaning to, but unable not to, prepared to look away the moment Aaron noticed. But he never even glanced his way. Aaron waited for Russell to wrap up and pass it to him to run down the specials for the night. He looked at everyone *but* Bobby as he did. When he finished, he lit up while the non-smokers and those who'd had enough of the cold rushed the door to get back inside. The rest took their last drag, tossed the butts, and filed in. Bobby walked past Aaron with his head down, but

Aaron reached out for his wrist.

"Hang back a second," he said.

Michelle waited in the hallway just past the open door. The heat curtain above the doorway blasted and drowned out the sounds of the kitchen. Bobby waved her away. She gave an enthusiastic double thumbs-up and headed towards the front. Aaron released Bobby's wrist and the blood returned to his fingers. He stepped back and let the door latch shut.

Was this it? Had Aaron made up his mind about where Bobby had gone? Maybe he had figured out the truth about Bobby's father after all, though he couldn't see how, yet the frenetic speed at which the thoughts in Bobby's brain ran made any and all scenarios seem possible.

Remember, he said he wouldn't hurt you. Yeah, right. He bashed some kid in the face right out on the street and he didn't even know him and that kid never lied to him.

Bobby tucked his hands in a pocket in the front of his apron and ran his finger along the edges of the corkscrew of his wine key. If he got it out fast enough, he could jam it into the softest part of Aaron's face if he came at him.

The thought of it recalled the image of the boy lying in the street.

He let go of the corkscrew.

Seeing that had been enough violence to last him the rest of his life, and yet he stood not ten feet away from his best friend and was trying to think of the best way to take him out. Bobby's instincts had failed him up to now and he knew it. Maybe it was time to ignore them.

"Look, man," Bobby said.

Aaron brought his finger to his lips and shushed him. "You know what's weird?" he asked. "I can't quite get used to opening doors yet." He exhaled smoke from the corner of his mouth. "Who'd think that's a thing to get used to? Stepping out from one place to another just because you feel like it. Jesus, it's the simplest thing. We totally take it for granted, though. Going from this room to that one. Going outside. Closing the door to the bathroom. No more taking things for granted, Bobby. Not for one more second."

He reached behind his back and Bobby gripped the wine key again. Aaron brought back a white envelope and held it out in front of him. Bobby took it and eyed him while he opened it and found it full of twenties, fifties, and hundreds.

"What the hell is this?" Bobby asked.

"That," he said, blowing out another cloud of smoke, "is about three month's rent."

Bobby handed it back to him. "I'm not taking your hush money."

"Hush money?" he asked, laughing. "Who says that? You watch too much TV, dude."

"Oh my God," Bobby said, his volume raised. "I can't take this. I just can't fucking take this." He didn't know if he meant the money, or Aaron, or both.

"You can take it, because you need it. You and Isabel both. I had a stash of cash no one knew about before I went away."

"*Away*?" Bobby said. "You didn't take a long vacation, Aaron. You were in prison. This money is from selling drugs and selling drugs put you in prison. Exactly where what you did last night is going to put us both."

"You think I need you to tell me where I was?"

"Then why the hell did you do that to that kid?"

"Keep your fucking voice down."

Bobby stepped closer to Aaron and spoke through clenched teeth. Aaron's indifference made him angry and he forgot for a moment that he feared him. "You might have murdered that kid, Aaron, and you dragged *me* into it."

68

"Some of the guards inside were former cops," Aaron said. Bobby threw up his hands and walked away from Aaron. He paced in front of him, disgusted with what seemed to be another impending jailhouse rumination.

"I don't care about–" Bobby started.

"Shut up and let me finish." Bobby stopped pacing. "Do you know what they thought of monkeys like that little thug? Either inside there or outside in the world? Nothing. They thought *nothing* of them. Less than the shit you step on that gets stuck in between the cracks of your shoes, so bad that you have to take a butter knife to them to get it out before you toss them in the trash. They thought less of them than that. They'd turn their head the other way for a shiv in the shower room for less than you'd make on a Saturday night closing shift."

Bobby folded his arms to mask a shiver. He didn't want to know why Aaron knew that. His eyes burned and tears collected at the bottoms. Aaron must have sensed his fear. He walked to Bobby and laid his heavy hands on his shoulders.

"I know you're scared. It was a scary thing. I told you, I didn't want it to go down that way, but it had to." He tried to pull Bobby in for a hug, but Bobby shrugged his hands from his shoulders and walked to the other side of the dock. Aaron's arms remained suspended in his potential embrace, then dropped to his sides. He shook his head in disbelief.

"Is there a point to this story?" Bobby asked.

"Yeah, there is, Bobby," Aaron said. "Nobody's going to give a shit about that kid. Least of all me." He tossed the envelope back to Bobby. It smacked him on the chest and fell to the ground. "And nobody else will either if you keep your fucking mouth shut. Call it hush money if that's what it takes. You might not see it now, but I only did what I did for you. To help you."

"Help me?" Bobby laughed. "Jesus Christ, you're going to put me in prison with you."

"Yeah, that's not an option," Aaron said. "For me *or* you." He disappeared down the hallway as the heavy metal door swung shut behind him.

Bobby looked down at the envelope. A few of the hundreds poked from the opening and began to absorb moisture from the snow. He picked it up and fanned out the dry ones. Some of the bills were soft with age. Others looked so new as to be fake, closer to gray than green. They smelled like what he imagined people meant when they talked about a new car. Three months of dignity, maybe some sorely-needed rest, right there in his hands. Three months to let Isabel get some help that might stick. All he had to do was the only thing he'd ever done well, and that was keep his mouth shut. Lie. If he did, his shitty life stayed on its shitty trajectory to its shitty but predictable end. Hell, it might even get a little bit better.

Maybe Aaron was right. Maybe no one would care about that kid. Maybe he would have done to Bobby what Aaron did to him. Maybe worse. But that boy's mother would care. No matter how much of an asshole a kid becomes, a mother always wants him home. He heard Isabel's voice asking him again where he was last night. That boy's mother must have wondered why he hadn't come home, why the cops came to her door in the middle of the night, why someone would do that to her baby.

He opened the envelope again and counted the bills.

That kid didn't have to come after them like that, though. Right? He could have left well enough alone, let Aaron's insult slide, been the bigger man.

Bobby folded the knot of cash and shoved it in his back pocket as he walked back inside and swallowed hard around a lump of his own bullshit.

CHAPTER
SEVEN

Dishes clattered. The smell of boiling grease and sizzling meat turned Bobby's stomach. He wanted the sky to split and dump buckets of snow so they'd have to close early, and he could just go home, though to what, he knew all too well.

Nothing for me here, nothing for me there.

He walked past the hot window. Aaron glared at him as he placed food on the metal shelf in front of him. Michelle stood at the computer, bouncing on her toes. Ruddiness colored her cheeks, but the rest of her skin was a shade of olive, only slightly darker than Bobby. Her stocking cap removed, Bobby saw that the red in her hair was only the tips, like she'd dipped the ends in paint. The rest was jet black and buzzed close on one side. She had a tiny green stone in her left nostril and rows of silver hoops lining her ears.

"They just sat us," she said to him.

"Come on," he said.

They left behind the obscene shouts between servers and kitchen staff for the hum of the dining room at dinner rush. Bobby absorbed the energy of a busy night on the floor. He appreciated the opportunity to lose himself. The restaurant filled with people who avoided cooking a meal, who sat in public where they were forced to be polite before the weather trapped them inside with each other and removed that luxury. Bobby didn't judge them. Being here, he hid in plain sight, just like them.

Kids cried while servers sang tired birthday songs. The nine-to-fivers formed a horseshoe around the bar. Businessmen scarfed down cheap happy hour hot wings that were too old to sell on the regular menu.

Michelle and Bobby reached their section to find a table of five young black men going over menus.

"Seriously?" Bobby said.

"What?" Michelle said.

Bobby shook his head and directed Michelle to take their drink orders. He watched from the bus stand while she headed to the table. Bobby saw one of them wore mostly royal blue, and he thought again of the kid and his friend at the Original. Out for food, just like these guys, never suspecting one of their own might not go home with them. One of them watched Bobby watch them. Bobby diverted his own gaze out the window to the parking lot. When he glanced back, the guy held his stare.

He never did see the other kid's face at the Original.

That couldn't be him. He didn't see me, anyway. Couldn't have.

Michelle came back with pad in hand, menus under her arm, and a look of pride. They gave her the whole order and she wanted to put it in the computer. Bobby looked at her with doubt and swiped his key card to activate the POS.

"Did they want soup or salad?" he asked.

She clenched her jaw. "I forgot to ask," she said.

"And how did they want this burger done?"

"Crap."

Bobby hit the cancel button. "Look, we both know I'm not going to make shit from this table whether you screw it up or not."

"Excuse me?"

"I don't know what this job is for you, but this is how I eat. From now, if I say just get drinks, then just get drinks. Don't take the whole order like you know what you're doing. I can't afford it."

"Wait, why aren't you going to make shit from this table?"

"Don't be dumb."

Michelle pulled her chin back as if she'd been slapped. Bobby took the pad from her and they returned to the table. The kid stopped his stare as they arrived. Bobby's paranoia downshifted.

Michelle followed his lead the rest of the night. They didn't talk to each other unless they had to. As the evening progressed, the dinner crowd thinned out. Another wave of snow came through, but slower than the forecast had called for, the storm losing strength. Their last table lingered over drinks. Michelle came back from running food and leaned next to Bobby against the computer stand. The coupled waved and signaled for their check.

"Drop it off and restock the table tents," he told her. "I'll meet you up at the bar and we'll count out the tip share." She saluted and headed towards the table.

Up at the bar, the happy hour crowd had long gone. Only the barflies buzzed about, some to play trivia, while others argued about the Steelers and the Pens. Bobby pulled up a stool. He took his lighter from his back pocket and spun it on the bar. His feet bounced on the brass foot rail. He dreaded the end of the shift all night. Any time left alone to think sent his brain out of the sprinter's blocks again. Paul, the bartender washed draft glasses in the sink under the taps in front of him. Bobby signaled to him for a pack of cigarettes from the glass case behind him. He slid them across to him.

"Club soda?" Paul asked.

Bobby stared at the taps. Maybe just one beer. Something to quiet the noise. That's why Isabel did it, right? Too much static upstairs. It would be so easy. Drink the first one quickly, get past that bitterness, so the next one goes down smooth until things get numb. Despite his resurgent fear, Bobby realized he needed the anxiety to stay sharp, to be clear of mind because despite Aaron's assurances, what happened would not simply go away. He had to think his way out of this mess.

"Let's get crazy," Bobby said. "Throw a lime in there."

"Whoa, I hope you're not driving," Michelle said from behind him. She pulled up a seat next to Bobby and made a frame around his face with her hands in the air. "Let me see. It's not a religious thing. And you don't strike me as a violent drunk. So just a one-beer-queer, am I right? Can't handle getting your drink on?"

"How about it's none of your business?" Bobby held out his hand. She sighed, handed him the book full of closed-out checks, and reached in her apron pocket to give him a folded wad of cash.

"Look, I know I screwed up at first, but I got it together. Didn't I?" she asked. "I'm going to make you like me. I'm very likable."

Bobby ignored her and counted the money. She ordered a beer. Bobby counted again.

The money wasn't right. It couldn't be.

"Did something get stuck in your pocket?" he asked.

"Dude, I'm wearing stretch pants," she said.

He shook his head and counted once more. Paul came back with a drink and Bobby reluctantly slid the tip share over to him. Paul counted it and looked at Bobby and Michelle over the rims of his glasses.

"Come on, bro," he said. "Between the two of you?"

"Sorry, man," Bobby said, jerking his head towards Michelle. "Had the newbie. Plus, it was a little dark in my section tonight."

"What the hell does that mean?" asked Michelle.

A voice boomed off to the side. "It means y'all had to wait on too many niggas."

Bobby turned to see Darryl amble from the steps that led down from the smoking section. Darryl was the only black server in the bistro. Of which he was aware, at least. His shaved head shone under the recessed bulbs that lit the artificial antiques covering the walls of the upper level of the restaurant. He wore an oversized hooded sweatshirt, and his novelty pin-filled suspenders, draped over his shoulder at the end of his shift, clacked with every step of his long legs. He had a boisterous laugh, a thunderous voice, and no love lost for Bobby.

They'd trained for the floor together, though Darryl had been working there years before Bobby. First as a dishwasher, then a busser. Bobby applied for the floor with no experience and got the job. Still, Darryl showed him all the things he knew about the restaurant from years of working there. Showed him to how to burn the ice if someone dropped glass at the service bar. Secret stashes of pre-rolled silverware to finish a closing shift faster. They'd even had much in common. Sons of single mothers, making ends meet. Then one night, Bobby complained to Paul that he wasn't in the mood to wait on a table of black people after they'd asked him for clean silverware. He hadn't realized Darryl was standing behind him, waiting on a drink. He said nothing to Bobby. That night, or any that followed.

"This dude right here can't stand to wait on black folks," he said to Michelle. "He's right, though. Niggas don't tip."

"What? That's messed up," Michelle said to Darryl. She took a cigarette from Bobby's pack and lit up.

"No, really, help yourself," Bobby said.

"You're telling me," she said to Darryl, "that you think all black folks don't tip."

"Put it like this," he said. "I don't run my ass off when they get sat in my section."

"See?" Bobby said.

"You ever think that's why you don't get tipped?" she said.

"No," Bobby and Darryl answered together. They exchanged a brief glance, then looked away.

"Y'all are a trip," Michelle said. She turned to Bobby. "I mean, aren't you mixed?"

Bobby froze. Darryl went wide-eyed, his cheeks puffed out, full of beer. He swallowed hard and exploded into laughter, holding his sides and hooting. Bobby laughed hard, too, but he saw Michelle didn't buy it. Darryl put his arms around both of them. Bobby shrugged him off.

"Girl, please. You can't say that shit when I got a drink in my mouth." He pretended to catch his breath and wiped an imaginary tear from his eye. Then he frowned and leaned in close to Bobby's face and squinted in mock concentration. "You do got some black-ass lips, though," he said to Bobby. "She might could be on to something." He laughed again and walked back to his barstool. Michelle stared at Bobby.

"You're really not?" she asked.

"You're serious? Look at me."

"I am."

"Yeah, well maybe you need another drink."

"That's not a no."

Fingers and thumbs dug into Bobby's shoulders and massaged them. He turned to see Aaron and choked on his smoke. Aaron's cook's jacket hung tied around his waist and blood from raw meat stained his checkered pants pink in spots. He slapped Bobby on the back and sat down on the other side of him. How long had he been there?

"What's not a 'no'?" he asked Michelle.

"Look at this bullshit," Darryl said from his seat at the other end of the bar. Bobby breathed out, grateful for the reprieve. Sports Center was running clips of yesterday's proceedings at the O.J. trial. Darryl downed his beer and ordered another.

"How they going to act like this ain't all a total set-up?" he said.

"How do you figure it's a set-up?" Aaron asked Darryl.

Darryl looked back down the bar at Aaron, his face twisted as though something rotten passed under his nose. Darryl didn't like Aaron before he had gone to prison. He hated Aaron's old wannabe act, said it insulted him on behalf of all black folks. You might as well be running around here in black face, he told Aaron once. The new Aaron now resided on the opposite end of that spectrum, and it only served to intensify Darryl's animosity.

Bobby didn't like Darryl, but he understood his anger towards Aaron. Aaron had embarrassed Bobby often when they were growing up. He ridiculed him about the way he talked and dressed in the hopes that he would stop. It made Bobby wonder if this new Aaron was just another act, if he had adopted this persona just to survive. But maybe it wasn't. Perhaps Bobby had planted some idea that that festered inside him in prison. Like a seed, it needed attention, nurturing, the right environment to grow.

He might as well have swung that brick himself.

"You going to tell me a damn near fifty-year-old dude killed a woman and a grown-ass man at the same time?" Darryl asked. "With a knife? The fuck out of here."

"A retired fullback," Aaron said. "One of the greatest athletes of all time. Incredibly strong."

The barflies stopped their buzzing, eavesdropping. Paul

repeatedly wiped down the same section of the bar as he watched the volley back and forth. One patron, a white man in a wrinkled oxford and tie, loosened at the neck, picked up his clamshell cell phone from the bar and pulled up the antenna. He eyed the conversation between Aaron and Darryl while he pulled open the phone.

"Aaron," Bobby said, tugging at his elbow. Aaron pulled his arm away. His eyes stayed on Darryl.

"So, what," Darryl said, "he held the dude with one arm while he killed her with the other? Come on, man. All of this, it's the same old bullshit. Don't nobody like to see a nigger with money. Especially the police. O.J. running around in nice cars with a white woman on his arm like Jack Johnson up in this piece. And cops be pulling down what? Forty? Fifty thousand a year, if they lucky? Man, please. You know how I spell 'conspiracy'? L.A.P.D. Those niggas hate niggers."

Aaron scoffed. "Conspiracy? You can't be serious."

"You remember Rodney King?" Darryl asked. "That nigga was crawling on the ground and those cops beat him like he killed somebody."

"You remember Reginald Denny?" Aaron asked. "The guy was just driving his truck when those animals pulled him from it." He looked at Bobby while he talked. He fought a smile as if to keep from laughing.

"Wait, who?" Bobby asked.

"Reginald Denny," Michelle said. "The truck driver. He took a wrong turn off the Santa Monica freeway and ended up in the middle of the L.A. riots. He got pulled from his semi and somebody hit him in the face with a brick."

Bobby stared at Aaron. Aaron winked at him.

"So what you saying?" Darryl asked Aaron.

"What I'm saying," Aaron said, "is you can't demonize an entire police force because of what a handful of cops did. Cops that were acquitted, by the way. You know what that means, right? Cleared of wrongdoing."

"Demonize?" Darryl asked. "They let you read in the joint?"

"But it's fair to demonize an entire race based on the actions of criminals?" Michelle asked.

Aaron turned and smirked at her. "Check your facts, sweetie. One of your people who attacked Denny was a process server. No criminal record. But the looting and violence got that blood of his up, and he just couldn't deny his DNA. None of them can. They stole from their own businesses. Attacked their own people. So do me a favor and flex your sociology minor somewhere else, okay? Men are talking."

As Aaron ranted, Bobby lit matches and tossed them in the ashtray. He prayed for a kitchen fire, a power outage, someone to come in and rob the place, anything to shut Aaron up or things were going to get bad in a hurry. He'd taken his eyes off the man with the phone.

"What about Bobby Green?" Michelle asked Aaron.

"Who?" Aaron asked.

"The man who drove Denny to the hospital when he saw him lying the street. The *black* man. Was that in his DNA? To risk his life for someone he didn't even know? Maybe *you* need to check *your* facts, sweetie."

Aaron's smirk disappeared. He leaned back in his seat and gave Michelle the once over. "So what are you, exactly?" he asked her.

"What?"

"I mean, you're not white, clearly" he said. "But all that shit in your face and the hair. It's got me a little confused."

Darryl pointed at Bobby. "You better get your boy."

"Guys," Paul said.

"I'm a human being," Michelle said.

Aaron sipped his beer and shrugged. "Half of one, maybe," he said. "Still doesn't count."

Michelle laughed in disgust. Darryl stood up.

Shit, here we go. Bobby looked across the bar again. The man with the phone looked towards the entrance to the bistro.

Michelle put her hand up to Darryl. She shook her head to signal it wasn't worth it. Aaron smiled at him. Just like he did to the kid at the Original. Bobby pulled at him. "Man, I think we'd better leave." Aaron ignored him.

"Keep smiling at me with them pretty white teeth, dude," Darryl said. "They new, right? You got them from the state, huh? Yeah, they do that for you bitches in the joint."

Darryl smiled. Aaron didn't.

"What, you didn't know?" Darryl asked Bobby. "You had to notice. Those teeth ain't his. My cousin was in lock-up with your boy there. Yeah, nigga, I know all about you."

Aaron turned away from Darryl. He hunched over his beer and swirled the glass on the ring of water in which it sat. Darryl saw he had Aaron on the ropes and moved in.

"Leave him be, man," Bobby said. "We get it."

"See, Bobby, you can't bite down on a dick in your mouth if you got no teeth," Darryl said. "The brothers busted them shits out his first day in. Saw through that weak-ass wannabe-a-nigga bullshit, didn't they? You just got a little too cute. Tried to act hard and shit. Way I heard it, they passed you around the first week. Used that mouth like a pussy."

Aaron bit his lip and stared into his glass while everyone at the bar watched at him. He withdrew, as small as the day he went to prison, tucked in on himself like he did in the truck. For an instant, Bobby forgave him for what he did to the kid. He almost understood it. He saw the scrawny loud-mouthed friend who was the brother he never had, and he cringed with every insult Darryl tossed at him. That Darryl's words affected him like that made Bobby think that maybe, just maybe there was something left of Aaron that he remembered. If Darryl could get to him, maybe Bobby could get through to him to find some way out of the mess he'd gotten them into. Darryl's humiliation wasn't having the effect he wanted. Not on Bobby. The verbal abuse made him feel defensive of Aaron. Even Michelle looked embarrassed for him.

"Okay, that's enough," Michelle said to Darryl.

"Whatever," Darryl said and turned to go back to his seat. "Fuck him."

"What happened to him?" Aaron said, his eyes still on his beer.

"What?" Darryl asked.

"Your cousin. What happened to him?"

"What you mean, what happened to him? Who said something happened to him?"

Aaron removed the hand that covered the spider-web tattoo on his elbow. He looked up at Darryl and covered his mouth. "Oops. Guess you hadn't heard everything."

It was the second time Bobby had seen that face on Aaron. It was the look he saw after he bricked the kid, after he leaned back in the passenger seat with a cigarette and calmly directed them home.

Satisfaction. Pleasure.

All the understanding rushed away. Aaron had crushed that kid's face because he wanted to. Not because he felt threatened. Not out of some need to protect Bobby. He was drunk and that kid mouthing off thought he was dealing with two scared white boys, when only one of them was white, and he wasn't the one who was scared. Maybe there had been a time when Aaron felt ashamed about what happened to him in prison, but that time was gone, and so was Aaron. If what Darryl said was true, what happened to Aaron in prison shattered him into unrecognizable pieces and violent bigots took him in and put him back together, but they fucked up the pieces and forced them to fit where they didn't. Aaron faked embarrassment while Darryl laid into him. He baited him just like he did that kid. That face he made sealed it. The Aaron Bobby knew was gone, and he knew then for certain that whatever thing had grown inside Aaron had lashed out and ensnared Bobby, pulling him behind his wake.

Darryl walked towards Aaron with his fists tight. Aaron finished his beer and stood. Bobby stood in between them, hands out to keep them separated. Paul ran to the outside of the bar to put himself between the two of them as well. Michelle shouted for them to stop. Paul put his hands on Darryl's chest. Darryl batted them away and Paul pushed him again. Some of the other staff that sat at the bar rushed the scene.

"You better be bullshitting," Darryl shouted over the barrier of people.

"Am I?" Aaron shouted back. "Look at me, Darryl. Am I?"

"Aaron, shut the fuck up!" Bobby yelled.

"Listen to your boy," Darryl said. "Faggot."

Aaron snorted and spit at Darryl. The glob landed on Darryl's cheek.

The sound sucked out of the room. Darryl wiped his face. Bobby, Michelle, Paul, stood inanimate, arms out to the side, fingertips spread, braced against nothing but the electric air.

"Okay," Darryl said.

He lunged. Paul dipped under his outstretched arms and wrapped his own around Darryl's body. The rubber soles of his boots squeaked on the polished hardwood as Darryl drove forward for Aaron.

"Let him go!" Aaron said to Paul.

Bobby held Aaron back, too. Michelle stood between Paul and Bobby, arms outstretched, Samson-like, hands on their backs, screaming for them both to stop. Bobby grunted and squinted with the effort. His eyes opened at the sound of the doors to the foyer swinging open.

Two white police officers, dressed in cold weather gear, bounded up the three steps to the bar area. One pushed back Michelle, Bobby, and Aaron, while the other peeled Paul from Darryl. Paul stepped away with his hands raised. The officer stood less than a foot from Darryl, one hand in front of him with an admonishing finger raised, the other hovering near his hip.

"What's the problem?" he asked Darryl.

"What you asking me for?" Darryl said, incredulous. "Ask that bitch." He pointed at Aaron. Bobby turned to look at Aaron. The rage in his face gone. The fanned neck, the wild eyes, contained. The officer glanced over his shoulder, past his partner to Aaron. Aaron shrugged, palms up in confusion. The officer turned back to Darryl.

"I'm asking you," he said. "And watch your mouth."

"This motherfucker spits in my face and I got to watch my mouth?"

The officer grabbed him by the wrist and spun him towards the railing surrounding the bar. The force made Darryl's hands shoot out and grip the rail. The officer grabbed him by the ribs and kicked his feet out to the sides. He patted him down.

"I don't believe this shit," Darryl said.

"I told you to watch your mouth," the officer said. He wrenched Darryl's arm behind him and Darryl shouted.

"He didn't do anything!" Michelle said.

Russell ran up from the kitchen, wet at the pits and out of breath. "What the hell is going on?"

"We got a call about a disturbance," said the officer standing in front of Michelle, Bobby, and Aaron. "You the manager?"

"I am." He pointed past the officer to his partner, who clicked shut the cuffs on Darryl's wrists. "Why is he under arrest?"

"The call said he'd become violent with another patron here, sir. Then he put his hand in my face and became belligerent." He yanked Darryl upright.

"That's bullshit!" Michelle said. She pointed at Aaron. "He spit at Darryl!"

"Why would I do that?" said Aaron. "I was minding my own business when he started berating me."

"Oh, my God, he's lying." She looked at Bobby. "Tell them."

Bobby looked at the floor, then to the bar. All those whose eyes had been locked on the situation now looked elsewhere. Everyone wanted to watch the action while it happened, but now that consequences loomed, they all turned away when Bobby's eyes met theirs. A short, quiet laugh escaped.

"It was just an argument. Nothing happened." He kept his head bowed, though the glares were almost palpable.

"We've just got a misunderstanding here, officers," said Russell. "Would you please let that young man go?"

The officer separating them from Darryl looked back to his partner and nodded. He rolled his eyes and pushed Darryl at the shoulder, turning him. He took a key to the cuffs.

"Whatever happens," he said to Russell, "it's on you."

"Understood," Russell said. "Thank you."

"You see?" the officer said to Darryl, spinning the loose cuffs once around his finger. "Polite. That's how you talk to people." He walked towards his partner and they headed towards the steps leading away from the bar. Darryl kneaded his shoulder and moved his arm back and forth.

"Yeah, whatever man."

Russell clenched his jaw. "Darryl, shut up."

The officer called out without looking back. "You watch that mouth of yours, son. It's going to get you in trouble." The doors closed behind them. Darryl pointed to Aaron.

"Outside," he said.

Aaron opened his mouth to respond, but Russell spoke first.

"Like hell," Russell said. "Darryl, get your shit, and let's go."

"What? Why I got to leave?"

"Oh, you're both out of here, but you're not fighting in my parking lot. I'm walking you out to your car to make sure you leave." He gestured to Aaron. "And then it's your turn."

Darryl snatched his belongings from the bar. Russell guided him by the elbow. Aaron stood as they approached. Russell stopped in front of him, placing himself between Aaron and Darryl. He stepped closer to Aaron, the space between them mere inches. Bobby eyes bounced back and forth between them. Aaron was a head taller than Russell and looked at him from underneath lazy eyelids, a crooked smile creasing the corner of his face.

"Sit your ass down before I call your P.O." He looked over Aaron's tattoos. "You think I don't know what all this shit means? I should have them send you back. It wouldn't take much." He took a small step closer. "But I know why you have all this ink." Aaron's smirk disappeared. "I know what men like you have to do to survive in there. And I don't want to send you back to that. So I'm telling you now, and that's the last time I'm going to tell you. Watch yourself."

Russell took Darryl outside. Bobby watched Aaron. He looked shaken. Darryl threw insults like a boxer going for the head, looking for the one-shot knockout blow. But Russell's quiet words landed like a shot to the liver, a pain localized at first, that echoed along neurons and synapses until they reached the brain and told the body to go down. Don't suffer anymore.

Russell re-entered within minutes and told Bobby and Aaron to go. Aaron offered no resistance. Bobby took his apron and gave the closed-out checks to Michelle. She reached for them, automatic in her movement, dazed from what had transpired.

"Hell of a first night, huh?" Bobby said with a weak smile. Michelle snapped to. She narrowed her eyes as she took the checks from his hand.

"Sincerely," she said, "go fuck yourself." She threw the checks onto the bar, turned her back to Bobby and took her seat. Bobby watched her back for a moment, then followed Aaron down the steps.

Outside the snow fell light but steady. Plow trucks scraped the parking lot clean. Salt crunched under Aaron's boots as he walked towards the rear parking lot. Bobby called after him to wait up. The pickup chirped and his taillights winked and he walked around to the passenger's side door. He pulled it open, popped the glove compartment, and retrieved the gun he'd gotten from Cort the night before. Pressure filled Bobby's chest.

"Aaron, what are you doing?"

Aaron paced the length of the truck. "They think they can talk to me like that? Any of them? Russell thinks he knows me?" Aaron's fingers gripped and released the gun. "He wants to know, I'll show him."

"Enough!"

Bobby's shout echoed throughout the parking lot. Aaron stopped pacing. His arms hung by his side. Bobby ran his hands over his face and moaned into them in aggravation.

"What are you doing, man? First that kid and now you're going to shoot someone? You're going to walk in there and just murder Russell, or whoever? Who are you, man?"

"Who am I? Who the fuck are you, dude?" His temples pulsed with each contraction of his jaw muscles. "You don't stick up for me in there? You don't have my back, now, after all this time?" He held the gun sideways and jabbed it in the air towards Bobby. "You don't defend yourself when that bitch says you're half nigger? Nah, fuck that."

Aaron stepped to move around him but Bobby put his hand on Aaron's chest. He stopped. Bobby looked to his gun hand. It shook. Fear? Anger? He pushed against Bobby's hand but only just. It would have been nothing for him to overpower Bobby, to shove him aside. But there he stood. As if he wanted to be stopped.

"Aaron. Come on, man. Please." He stopped pushing against Bobby's hand. Bobby cautiously lowered his arm but every muscle in his body felt ready to act, although to do what, he hadn't the slightest idea. Aaron breathed hard and fast. Then, with one forceful breath out, he calmed. His shoulders eased away from his ears. The throbbing at his temples faded.

"I was just trying to protect you, man. Last night. Just like you always did for me."

"No, man," Bobby said. "You don't get to do that. You are not going to make this about me." Heat roiled in his stomach and rose, swelled, easing the tension in his chest, relaxing the hold on his throat, melting his fear. He stepped aside. "You know what, go ahead. If you want to go in there and shoot him, shoot everyone, fuck it, man, go to town. I can't stop you. But don't you for one more second put this on me. You shoot him, it's because *you* want to. You think you're protecting me, you're dragging me deeper into a hole that neither of us can climb out of."

He stared at Bobby and held the gun by his side.

"Just put it away, man," Bobby said. "Please."

Aaron walked back to the truck and replaced the gun. He came back with his hands in his pockets like a scolded child.

"I'm sorry," Aaron said.

"For what, Aaron? I mean do you even know?"

"You never answered my question."

"What?"

"Time was you couldn't stand these people, Bobby. You used to give me a lot of shit for the way I was, but you always had my back. Always."

Bobby stayed silent.

"Do you have my back, Bobby? I need to know."

"Sure, man. Of course."

Bobby heard Isabel's false reassurance in his answer. Aaron's half nod indicated he heard it, too.

"Come on, I'll give you a ride home."

Aaron walked around to the driver's side. Bobby remained at the foot of the bed and looked at the truck. Aaron stood at the open door. He beckoned Bobby in with a tilt of his head.

"Hey, man, it's been a day, okay? The bus is going to be here any minute. I need a little time to myself, to clear my head. Shake this night off. That all right?"

Aaron narrowed his eyes, then nodded.

"You're cool, right? You're going to go home? This is done?"

Another nod. Slight.

"Cool," Bobby said. He walked up and gave Aaron an awkward slap on the shoulder, then jogged down the hill towards the bus stop. He turned for one last quick look over his shoulder.

Aaron lingered at the open truck door, watching.

CHAPTER
EIGHT

Robert awoke on his side of the bed. The expanse of the California king remained untouched, even after a year. They used to begin their evening in the middle, always with the best intentions of falling asleep, Robert the larger spoon. Amorous ideas sometimes kept them from falling asleep that way, often retreating to their cooler sides of the bed, connected at the hands. Other times, the futility of Robert finding comfortable "other arm" placement or Tamara's impossible metabolism generating furnace-like heat kept them from remaining curled into each other. They laughed together at the hopelessness of it. But they never stopped trying.

After showering and dressing, he made his way downstairs. He padded barefoot, almost past the closed French doors to the dining room, then stopped. He pulled them shut as if to close in the divorce papers that sat on the table, like placing a lid on a jarred candle, depriving the flame of oxygen so it might flicker out of existence. Yet there they sat. Untouched and unmoved. Waiting.

He kept walking.

It was a slow shift in the ER. Mostly slip and falls, some of the city's homeless seeking refuge from cold exposure. Nothing to necessitate the trauma team's intervention. Robert had long ago abandoned the guilt of wishing for work, the gallows mentality that accompanied the enjoyment of his job. It was a necessity, a way to disconnect from the visceral nature of the task at hand. Still today, he wished for it for considerably more selfish reasons. Unoccupied, his mind continued to drift towards the paper on the table. How could she have already signed? Were they truly past all discussion? How had he earned such spite? Robert knew the answers to his questions and the need for distraction swelled.

Night came, and towards the end of his shift, Robert took the stairs to the ICU to look in on Marcus Anderson, the assault victim from the previous night. It had taken all the king's horses and men to put him back together again. Titanium plates reinforced the shattered bone of his orbital, but he had lost the eye, the void covered by gauze and surgical tape. They pulled a number of splintered teeth and wired his jaw shut. The bleed in his brain caused increased pressure within his skull, so they removed a section of it. Robert pressed his lips together as his mind tried to fill in the negative space the craniotomy left in Marcus. God called him home in pieces.

It was unclear yet if he would survive. His EEG read dismally. If he did live, he would be in agony. He would eat his meals through straws for months. If he regained the ability to talk, his speech would never be the same. His driver's license showed a handsome young brother with a winning smile. A plastic surgeon wouldn't touch him without good insurance, of which his family had none. Lorraine had told Robert that when they visited. His mother's hand had hovered over his face, not wanting to touch the bruising and swelling that would likely end as a ruin of scar tissue. Robert wondered if he and his team had saved the boy or damned him.

He thought of Tamara again. Thought about how they would have handled this as parents. Thought about the kind of mother she wanted to be, the kind she would have been. Maybe despite all the pain they felt now, they had, in some ways been spared.

Tamara didn't want children. She'd said so on their second date over the best filet Robert had ever had. They'd eaten at Donovan's in the Gas Lamp district. Her pharmaceutical company paid. She told him that children didn't figure into her career plan so he should get that idea right out of his head. He spit his wine back into his glass. She smirked at him. "You didn't know this was a date?" she'd asked.

"This isn't the part where I tell you I'm not interested in your product and you give me free samples?"

"Well now that you have, I can officially call this a business dinner and charge it to the company," she said. "But I would have gotten that out of the way on the first dinner with the rest of your practice."

"I figured this was just your method of divide and conquer," he said. "Picking us off one by one."

"Who's to say it isn't?" She winked. "I'll be getting your oldest partner in the sack tomorrow night. I love the smell of Bengay in the morning." Robert faked a dry heave and she laughed. "Besides, if you thought this was just another pitch, would you really have had dinner with me?"

"You promised filet. I have school loans."

"Fair enough." She raised her glass. Robert clinked it with his. "No kids," she said.

"You're assuming I even like you."

"You like me."

They talked for hours. She'd charmed him from her first sales call to the practice. After that dinner came many more. She was so different from the sisters Robert knew in school, from any he'd ever known. She didn't tell him he talked white for using proper grammar, likely because they both did. Robert saw himself on the high-yellow end of the spectrum while Tamara had a reddish tone to her light skin. Choctaw, she said, from Oklahoma, on her daddy's side, which caused her black hair to come to her shoulders long and straight. They empathized with each other about how tough it had been for them growing up the outcasts of the outcasts. They had been ostracized by their own people for being too white while they were mascots for their white friends, becoming the black friends they quickly pointed to when someone accused them of being racist. Even in California, she'd said, it had never been easy. It scared Robert, how much—and how quickly—he'd liked her. They went to bed together on that first date. It wasn't so unusual for Robert at the time, but the way he felt about her in the morning was. He wanted her to stay, and she did. They moved in together three months later. They married within the year.

Robert had lied about not wanting kids. He told himself she'd change her mind, that he just had to be patient, let it be her idea. Sometimes he introduced the idea as a joke, pointing out bratty kids in the grocery store, telling her how they'd handle them so much better. Most women would kill for a man who wanted to be a father, he told her. She reminded him she wasn't most women. She advanced quickly through the ranks of her company and had become a regional sales manager within a year. She traveled often and when she returned home, they wouldn't leave the bedroom most of the weekend. He'd roll off her and give an exaggerated sigh of exasperation as he peeled off the condom and tossed it in the bedside wastebasket. She smacked his damp bare chest with the back of her hand.

"Do you want me taking those pills and having a stroke?" she said.

"Your company sells them," he said. She rolled her eyes then turned on her side to face him, her head in the palm of her hand.

"Weekends like this? Poof." She blew into her hand and snapped her fingers. "At least until we'd be too old to enjoy it anymore." Robert wiped away a bead of sweat rolling down between her cleavage.

"You underestimate my libido," he said. "When I'm eighty and my frontal lobe is shot, I'll still be chasing you around with my pants around my ankles."

She pinched his nipple, then rolled away and walked to the bathroom for a shower. The high curve of her ass mesmerized him, like the natural pop in her hips that she exaggerated when she knew he watched her walk away. Shit, maybe she's right, he thought, and he jumped up to join her in the shower.

He caught glimpses of things beginning to change. They visited her sister in the hospital after she'd had her first child. Tamara was so thrilled to be an auntie. Her sister went to hand Tamara her new nephew after she'd finished nursing him, but Tamara waved her hands and pointed her sister towards Robert. She ignored her and placed the baby gently in Tamara's arms. Pure terror filled Tamara's eyes. Her nephew squeaked and grunted, the beginnings of a fuss. Tamara gently bounced and shushed him and his cries reached a pitch where Robert thought she might hurl the baby back to her sister when the bouncing finally shook loose a burp. Tamara laughed and the fussing stopped. When he opened his eyes, Tamara was completely his. She didn't give him back to her sister until it was time to go. Down the elevator and all the way back to the car, she went on and on about how she never wanted to do that again. How she felt like she was going to break him and why would her sister force him on her. All the while, she stole sideways glances at Robert. She wasn't doing it to see if he was listening. She wanted to see if he bought her story. He didn't. He hardly stopped smiling the entire drive home. Neither of them did, though she kept her head turned away from Robert to hide it.

A beautiful blonde with huge blue eyes named Abigail changed everything. Robert didn't know exactly what it was about her that did it. Maybe it was how she stood at a statuesque two feet tall. Maybe it was the way she climbed into his lap and tugged on his beard. Or maybe it was how she substituted her r's with w's. Whatever it was, that three-year-old had an undeniable charm. They had been invited to the home of Wyatt, one of the partners in Robert's practice. His wife, Denise, made a holiday dinner of roast leg of lamb with rosemary potatoes. Robert leaned into Tamara and whispered in her ear when Denise excused herself to fetch dessert.

"That white woman can cook." Tamara swallowed her wine down the wrong pipe and coughed.

Wyatt smiled at Robert. "Yes, she can."

Tamara gave Robert wide sideways eyes and he laughed uncomfortably. Just then, Abigail burst into the dining room through the sliding double doors. Her nanny ran behind her with arms outstretched, apologizing. Abigail wore a burgundy velvet dress with an oversized satin bow tied in the back. Its tails streamed behind her as she ran giggling around the table. Her father made a mock grab for her and she squealed in delight as she rounded the head of the table. She came up beside Robert and tugged at his slacks.

"Hi," she said, a little out of breath.

"Well, hello."

"Up," she said. She reached her arms up towards Robert. Tamara smiled and shrugged. Wyatt nodded his approval. Abigail grabbed at the air with impatient hands and a look that asked Robert what took him so long. He scooped her up and plopped her onto his lap. She leaned forward and gave Wyatt a raspberry. He waved his finger in false admonishment and her body shook with giggles. Denise called from the kitchen that she had too many pies to bring to them and to join her in the kitchen where the coffee brewed. Robert went to set Abigail down, but she wrapped her arms around his neck.

"You coming with me?" he asked.

"Mm-hmm," she said.

"Be careful," Tamara said to Abigail. "I'm a jealous woman."

Abigail looked over Robert's shoulder and stuck her tongue out at Tamara. Tamara hooted and clapped her hands together. Wyatt gave her a gentle scold and Abigail told Tamara "sowwy." Tamara forgave her and they all walked to the kitchen. The smell of warmed apples and cinnamon blended with the aroma of roasting beans. Denise had three different pies on the counter. A stainless steel espresso maker spit into porcelain cups lined up beneath it. Plush bar stools encircled the large island in the center of the kitchen. Before Robert sat, Abigail wiggled and wanted to be put down. Her legs scissored in the air before he set her down. She took off the moment her feet hit the ground and ran into the living room across from the kitchen. As they took their seats, Wyatt raised his wine glass and nodded to his wife to do the same.

"To new partners," he said.

Robert started to echo his toast before he registered what Wyatt had said. He looked over to Tamara. She held her glass in one hand while she covered her mouth with the other. Then she reached across to Robert and pressed up under his chin to close his mouth. She turned his head back towards Wyatt and Denise. They smiled and raised their glasses higher.

"To new partners," Robert said.

They all sipped. Wyatt walked around the corner of the island and extended his hand. Denise went the other direction and hugged Tamara. As Wyatt and Robert shook, Robert felt another tug at his slacks. He looked down to see Abigail again. She held a wooden puzzle board in her hands and raised it over her head.

"Up," she said again. Robert obliged and sat her on his lap. The puzzle had a number of farm animal cutouts. She turned it upside down and they hit the countertop with a clatter. She turned back to look at Robert. "You help?"

"I don't know," Robert said. "I'm not much of a surgeon."

"She never does this," Wyatt said. "I'll get her if she's bothering you."

Robert shook his head and helped Abigail replace the pieces. He pretended to be confused about where they went. Abigail guided his hands to the right spots. She clapped and squeaked when they fit. Robert laughed and looked across the island to where Denise had taken Tamara. Tamara had her hand pressed to her chest and her eyes shimmered.

"Are you okay?" Robert mouthed.

She pressed her lips together and nodded. "I love you," she mouthed. Robert blew her a kiss.

After four bottles of wine, Wyatt called a car service to take them home. Tamara pawed at Robert in the backseat. He kept his eyes on the driver's in the rearview and kept pushing her hand to the side. They laughed the whole way. She pouted at the rejection of her advances and walked her fingers across the seat and up Robert's leg. She attacked when they reached the door to their apartment complex. Their tongues darted in and out of each other's mouths. Robert fished in his front pocket for his keys and she grabbed his crotch. They stumbled through the open door and clumsily tried to keep their mouths connected, their teeth clicking together as they walked in-step to the elevator. The doors opened and she pushed him up against the mirrored interior wall. She loosened his belt and reached down the front of his pants. He gave a playful laugh at her aggression and she gently bit his lower lip. The doors opened on the third floor and she led him by the hand into the hall. He bunched his pants at the waist with his other hand and followed her lead.

She let go and made it down the hall before Robert. The door to their apartment stood open, and her dress and heels sat in a heap in the foyer. He rounded the corner and walked towards the bedroom. Tamara lay naked on the bed, propped on her elbows, legs crossed at the ankles. Robert loved the way her breasts fell to the sides when she lay like that. She beckoned him with a finger. He let his pants drop around his ankles and shimmied towards her, his arms out, hands groping at the air like he'd promised he'd do as a geriatric. She tossed her head back with laughter and covered her mouth when she snorted. Robert stripped off the rest of his clothes. She slid herself back up towards the head of the bed and he crawled after her. They kissed again as he pressed against her, then he stopped and sighed. She tried to hold on to him as he rolled off her over towards the nightstand and pinched a condom between two fingers. He brought the wrapper to his teeth. Tamara climbed on top and took it from his mouth and tossed it to the side.

"Uh-uh," she said. He reached in the drawer for another one. "Hey," she said. "Stop."

"You're drunk. So am I."

She took the condom from his hand and threw it on the floor. She grabbed his face and made him meet her eyes, then reached down and put him inside of her.

Sunlight peered around the edges of their midnight shades the next morning. They fell asleep naked and spooning. Her breast cupped in his hand. The inside of his eyes felt like flypaper and he wanted them to stay shut, dreading the hangover perched on the edges of his skull, waiting for him to sit up so it could attack. He pushed his nose into the back of her head and inhaled. Her hair smelled of hibiscus. She pushed her hips back and he met them with his, then she reached back and kneaded at his neck. She always pinched just a little too hard so the edges of her nails pricked his skin, but he didn't mind.

"So," he said.

"Yes, I remember."

"And you're okay with it? I mean, light-skinned as we are, the thing might end up an albino." She turned and slapped his chest, laughing. She brought her nose to his and he talked through pursed lips. "My breath is bad."

She scrunched up her face. "Yeah it is."

Robert sucked his teeth and turned her by the shoulders, so they spooned once again. "You're certain about this?"

She rolled to face him again. "Let's do it again. Just to be sure."

The night nurse pushed open the door to Marcus's room. Robert snapped to and cleared his throat. She smiled politely as he stepped away from the bedside, out of her path to Marcus's bedside to record his vitals and change his IV bag. Robert checked his watch to see he'd been standing there for almost fifteen minutes. He'd hoped a visit with Marcus would distract him. What a false hope it had proven to be. His shift over, he walked down the stairwell back to the emergency department and out the entrance doors. A payphone hung attached to the outside wall. He lifted the phone from the cradle and dropped in a few coins. When his answering machine picked up, he entered the code to retrieve his messages. Two loud beeps signified he had none. He hung up. The coins rattled and slid in the metal trough as he walked back towards the doors.

In the locker room. Robert changed out of his scrubs into slacks and a pressed shirt. Once again outside, he lit a cigarette. A second round of snow pushed its way into the city. The fresh layer reflected the light of the streetlamps and a steady whoosh carried in the air as though the sky breathed. He shoved his hands in his topcoat pockets. He'd missed Pittsburgh winters, and without the slicing winds. It was a nice night for a walk. He started off in the direction of Lou's. He had a bill to settle.

CHAPTER
NINE

sabel hated lying to Bobby, especially because she was so bad at it, and he knew it. She heard the doubt in his voice as loudly as the door he had slammed on his way out when she said she'd pick up the double. She had only half lied. It would be no problem to send someone home on the breakfast shift, but there was no telling what time Robert might come back to pay his tab. He would. That much she knew. As long as they had known each other, he would never be anyone's stereotype. There was no doubt he'd be back to pay that tab, and then some. Because she could count on him returning, she couldn't chance missing him. There was only one hospital so close to Lou's, but if she staked him out there, chances were she'd frighten him. No, this had to seem accidental, a chance encounter that felt unplanned, and on his terms.

Throughout her shift, she thought about what she might say. While taking an order, she wrote "eggs scrambled been a long time" on her pad. She forgot refills, dropped plates, and spilled hot coffee on herself. Pockets pulled her aside and asked if her she'd been drinking.

I wish, she thought. She wouldn't have been so Goddamned nervous.

She assured him she hadn't in a tone terser than she'd intended, and Pockets gave her that same doubtful look that Bobby had perfected over years of disappointment. Any other day, his condescension would have angered her. Not today. The excitement and anxiety and fear left no room for anger. At least not for him.

She pulled up to Lou's just before six o'clock and turned off the car. The Fox coughed a death rattle, then quieted. Isabel pulled down the visor and checked her teeth for lipstick stains. Her white blouse had a plunging neckline with ruffles down the side that was tight around her middle but still fit if she left it untucked. She tucked it and untucked it again, hating how dated the shirt was and that it was the nicest one she owned. She untucked it one more time and told herself that Robert was no one she needed to impress. Then she laughed at herself.

"Yeah, right," she said.

She refreshed her lipstick and reached for the door. She stopped. Cold fingers walked the back of her neck and slid their tips down her arms.

You're right back where you promised you wouldn't be, and in more ways than one. Did you forget why it's been twenty years?

"No," she said.

You told Bobby no more drinking. You told yourself no more Robert. Not after how he treated you.

"I'm not going to drink," she said. "I'm going to sit there, sip club sodas like a good girl, and wait. This is happening for a reason. There has to be a reason."

Who are you here for? Bobby? Or you?

"I'll wait here," she said. "I'll keep my head down and wait until I see him go in. Then I'll arrange for him to meet Bobby and I'll leave."

A knock on the passenger side window made her jump. One of the regulars waved and asked if she was coming in. She cursed to herself and waved back. There's no way he'd go in without telling Nico he'd seen her. She gripped the steering wheel.

"Club sodas," she said. "No sweat."

Who are you here for?

"I don't know."

Nico had a vodka tonic waiting on the bar when she walked in.

"Two nights in a row? To what do we owe the pleasure?" Isabel pulled up her usual seat. The drink fizzed as an ice cube floated from the bottom and bobbed on the surface. It *would* calm her down, let her relax. She wrapped her fingers around the glass and pushed it towards Nico.

"Thanks, hon," she said. "I'm still a little queasy from last night."

"You sure? Might take the edge off that dog bite."

"I'm good. Club soda." She took off her jacket and hung it on the back of the stool. Nico whistled.

"Look at you," he said. "You redd up good, huh? That for me?"

"Maybe."

He placed a club soda in front of her. "Seriously, what's got you here so early looking so jazzed up?"

She hadn't thought that part through, what to tell Nico. "I felt bad how I ducked out of here last night. I didn't want you to think it was you," she said. Nico smiled. He bought it. "Speaking of which, that guy ever come back and pay his tab from last night?"

"No. Shocker, right? Prick." Isabel breathed out and took a sip from her seltzer. She settled in and waited.

Every time the door opened, her heart beat a little faster. The snow let up enough that more of the natives and regulars decided to come flatten their asses at the bar. Hours passed and no Robert. She talked with the locals, and the drunker they got, the closer they leaned. Over the odors of salted nuts and day-old pretzels on their breath wafted the sweet-sour smell of liquor and it pulled at her. The top shelf bottles were lit from underneath, as if on display just for her. Her head throbbed. She checked the clock again. Nico was right. Robert wasn't coming. She hadn't known him as well as she'd thought. How embarrassed she felt, how ridiculous this all was. She massaged her temples.

"You all right?" Nico asked. "You're looking kind of green again."

"Gee, thanks."

"I mean don't get me wrong, you make it look good."

"Think I'm going to pack it in, stud. This isn't exactly the best place to stay on the wagon."

"And I'm here offering you drinks. Now who's the prick?"

"Forgiven, hon. I owe you for the soda?" Nico waved it off. She sucked the soda down to the bottom when someone sat down next to her. He smelled terrific. And familiar.

"A little busier in here than last night," he said to Isabel. He looked older up close. A little more tired than he did the night before. God damn if it wasn't him and what the hell did she do now but go for it.

"I know you," she said. Her voice cracked and he turned all the way on his stool to face her. He narrowed his eyelids and smiled that smile that said he was trying to be polite and figure out how to get her to tell him her name without having to ask. Isabel knew he knew her from last night, yet he still didn't *know her*. Before he could speak, Nico tapped the bar.

"You forgetting something?" Nico asked. Robert opened his wallet and brandished a credit card. He asked Nico to start a tab.

"He'll take a Glen Fiddich, neat," Isabel told Nico. Robert leaned back and gave her the once over. "I'll take another club soda, too."

Nico snatched Robert's credit card from the bar and fired seltzer into Isabel's glass until it brimmed over. He set Robert's drink on the bar hard and glared at them both as he made his way to the other end of the bar.

"I don't think he likes me," Robert said. Isabel raised her glass to him and took a quick sip because she was going to say something stupid like "I like you" and mess up this whole thing and she told herself to slow down because her brain was off to the races again. "You look nice tonight," he said.

"I didn't last night?" she asked

"I guess I could have phrased that better," he said.

"You look nice, too."

"So how do you know my drink?"

This is why you got dressed up? For someone who has no idea who you are. Is it coming back to you now why you never told him?

"You really don't remember me?" Isabel asked.

"Outside of last night?" She nodded. "I'm sorry, I'm embarrassed to say I don't."

"Not *that* embarrassed," Isabel said, "not as easily as that came out."

He smiled and cocked his head in agreement and went to take another sip. He looked at her when he lowered his glass and set it back down on the bar. She couldn't take his pretending to try and remember anymore.

"Bobby, it's Isabel," she said.

"Wow," he said. "Bobby. Nobody's called me that in a long time." He took another sip, then his eyes widened. "Wait, wait, wait," he said. "Izzy Saraceno?"

She failed to hide her smile. "Nobody's called *me* that in a long time."

"Wow. Wow! God, I haven't thought about that name in ages. It's been, what, twenty years?"

"Twenty-two."

"Who's counting, huh?" he asked. He shook his head again. "Still Saraceno?" She raised her left hand and wiggled her bare ring finger. "Surprising," he said.

"Why?"

"Honestly?"

"No, I'll take the bullshit, please."

"I don't know," he said. "I'm still kind of mortified about not recognizing you right away and it felt like the right thing to say."

"I think I would have preferred the bullshit."

They laughed. Robert shifted in his seat and looked down into his drink while Isabel stared. Their silence made the quiet din of the bar seem much louder. He glanced at Isabel out of the corner of his eye and back to the bar. She knew she gawked at him but she couldn't stop. She had to sit on her hand to keep from reaching out and touching him to make sure he was real. She needed to know where he'd been all these years, why he was here now. More than that, she wanted to know why he looked so sad.

"You want to talk about it?" she asked

He turned his drink in place on the counter and kept his eyes fixed on it. In him she saw her son, home from grade school, playing with his food at dinner, upset about a girl who didn't circle "yes" on a note asking her to "go with him" and her anger and desire for Robert pendulumed.

"About what?" he asked.

"It's been two decades," she said. "Pick something"

"You'd have to charge me for the therapy."

She smirked. "We can work something out."

"I appreciate it, but I'm good." He tilted his head back to finish his drink and asked Nico for the tab.

"You're leaving?" Isabel asked.

"Yeah, it's late and I've got an early day tomorrow."

"It's not that late," she said. She heard the desperation in her voice and took a deep breath. "One more," she said. "One more with me and I'll let you live down not recognizing me."

"That was bad, wasn't it?" he asked. Isabel mock grimaced and nodded. Robert laughed. "One more," he said.

Isabel stood, rocked on her heels, and grinned. "There's a booth back there," she said.

Robert ordered another scotch and Isabel asked for the vodka tonic. Nico brought it and shot Isabel a look that she pretended not to see it as she guided Robert towards the rear of the bar. The red vinyl squeaked as they slid into either side of the booth. Robert pulled out a pager from his front pocket and set it on the table. He hit a button and the small screen lit up a yellowish-green.

"Expecting a call?" she asked. The sadness returned to his face.

"No," he said. "I'd like to be, but I don't think I am."

A loud crack echoed behind them from a break on the pool table. Isabel noted the gold band on Robert's finger because he kept sliding it back and forth, almost off, never fully on. She wondered if the person who gave him that ring was the person he hoped would call.

"How long have you been married?" she asked.

"Depends."

"On?"

He corkscrewed the ring up and down his finger and stared at the palm of his hand. "On who you ask," he said.

Isabel took a pull on the straw in her vodka tonic, and that smooth burn hit her, a quick shot of comfort that helped contain her simultaneous anger at and longing for him.

"You sure you don't want to talk about it?" she asked.

"I do," he said. He lifted his head to look at her and he glanced at her cleavage before meeting her eyes. Isabel noticed and leaned in and put her elbows on the table, seeing if she could get him to do it again. He didn't. "But I'm not going to."

"Why not?"

"Look, I don't want to be rude, but we haven't seen each other for the better part of two decades. We were kids. I don't know you like that now. I shouldn't be sharing something like this with someone like you."

A burning in her ears and cheeks consumed the soothing warmth the vodka produced just a moment ago.

"Excuse me? Someone like me?"

"That came out wrong. I meant talking about issues at home with a woman with whom I had a relationship. That's not fair to my wife."

Isabel laughed in disbelief. "When did you ever care about fair? And you call what we had a relationship?"

"Would you mind keeping your voice down?"

Robert's eyes glanced around the bar and past Isabel. Isabel looked over her shoulder to see some patrons straining to listen without looking like they were.

"Wow, nothing changes, huh, Bobby? Still don't want to be seen in public with me, after all this time. Any other girl, sure, but not me. Don't you talk to me about fair."

"What are you talking about?"

"How many nights, Bobby? How many did we spend in your apartment? Never going out, to a restaurant, dancing, any of it. Always pizza or Chinese, late at night, watching television until you got me into bed and left before dawn. And yet I stuck around, because I thought if I put my time in, you'd maybe like me enough to love me. To show me on your arm. I'd convinced myself until..."

Do not tell him in anger, she told herself. She breathed deep and closed her eyes, blinking a tear down her cheek.

"I came to find you on campus one afternoon. I needed to talk to you. I found you in the game room in the quad with some other bitch hanging all over you while you shot pool with your boys. I knew right then and there what I meant to you. You had no problem being seen with her. Hell, you two were practically making out on the table." She jutted her jaw and shook her head. "I was convenient for you, Bobby, until I wasn't. And I deserved better. So, I turned around and left and decided I'd never think about you again." Her voice cracked with that last utterance and she hoped he didn't realize that last part was only half true.

Robert folded his hands in front of him and dropped his head. *Damn right, you can't look at me.* Her breathing quickened. She'd waited so long to say those things, thought she'd never get the chance to say them, and there was an intense yet momentary relief at having said them. Momentary because she still had the most important thing yet left to say.

Roberts shoulders lifted and then dropped quickly with a heavy whoosh of his breath. When he looked up, he wasn't contrite. He seethed.

"You've got your nerve. You been holding on to that, excuse me, that bullshit, all this time?"

"Bullshit?"

"You heard me. That's one hell of a selective memory you have. How convenient for you that it allowed you to script me as the bad guy in whatever drama you built in your head."

"Hold on—"

"No, you hold on, Izzy. I liked you." He paused. "More than you knew. But I could never tell you that. Because I couldn't...no, I wouldn't, let myself get too close to you."

"Let me guess. Because you were scared, right? The idea of it was all just too terrifying? God, I'm so sick of men using that nonsense."

"You're Goddamned right I was scared, Izzy. You know why?"

Isabel leaned in and scrunched up her face. "Commitment? Giving up all the other tail?"

"Your father."

Isabel sat back.

"Those nights in my apartment that you disdain so much now? Clearly, and conveniently I might add, you're forgetting why we spent so much time there. You were living at home at the time. Are you forgetting what you told me about your father?"

Isabel's cheeks went prickly. She tucked a stray ringlet of hair behind her ear. "No, I remember."

"When we were seeing more of each other. When things got serious. Jesus, you laughed about it, Izzy. 'My Dad would answer the door with a gun if I came home with a black guy.' Like it was a game to you. Asked me if it wasn't more exciting knowing it was kind of dangerous. As if it wouldn't actually happen. You remember that part? Or is that too inconvenient?"

Isabel pressed her lips together and nodded.

"For Christ's sake, Izzy, the man was a retired cop. I didn't go out in public with you because, yes, I was terrified. I didn't know who you knew, and I damn sure didn't know who your father knew. But for you, it was like some adventure. Like I was some kind of forbidden fruit. Sure, you might catch hell if he found out, but that was the worst you had to fear. Not me. I had a hell of a lot more to be afraid of.

"I tried, Izzy, I tried really hard. All the nights we spent together might have been at my place, but if you remember, there were a lot of nights. Because despite how afraid I was, I honestly wanted to see if there was a way. But every minute I spent with you, I couldn't think about anything else but the consequences. Eventually, that got to be too much. I knew there was no future for us. I couldn't commit to that. So, I didn't."

He sipped his drink and looked off to the side. Isabel twirled her glass in the puddle of condensation beneath it, looking up only long enough to see if he was looking at her. When he turned back towards her, she dropped her chin again.

"Maybe I should have told you," he continued, "but a big part of me was so embarrassed. How could I be a man and tell you I was afraid? It was easier not to face it. I didn't want to be scared, to have who I loved be dictated by fear. Another part of me, though, wished that you'd realize what that fear must have been like for me. And yeah, I guess I was angry that you didn't, and so maybe being with the other girls was because I wanted you to feel some of that same hurt. It wasn't right, I know that, and for that I'm sorry. But only for that."

Robert blew out another rush of air. Isabel sat hands by her side, blinking back tears, looking off into nothingness in a post-concussive daze, rocked by the revelation.

He was right. About all of it.

She'd been selfish, unable to look past her own ability to not to have to think about the things he had no choice to, and in doing so, she made him the villain. A conscienceless lothario who didn't deserve to know about his child. She opened her mouth reflexively to apologize but no words seemed adequate. Robert looked at her expectantly, but she said nothing, only closed her mouth again.

"I should go," he said. He finished his drink and stood. "Look, despite all of that, it was good to see you again, Izzy. It really was." He put his coat on and paused. "I hope you have a nice life."

Izzy stared straight ahead, unable to look him in the eye, still wordless.

"I'll get the tab on the way out. You take care."

Isabel watched him stop at the bar and settle up with Nico.

You never asked him why he was back in town, or for how long. You just jumped down his throat for something that was your fault.

He's going to be gone again, and that's on you, too. He isn't for you anymore, but this isn't about you. Get off your ass.

She sprung up, banging her knee on the table, and fast-limped, holding on to it with one hand as she called out to Robert at the door.

"Robert, wait."

He turned to see her half-bent over, clutching her knee and hobbling towards him. He looked confused.

"That thing I needed to tell you back then? I still need to tell you."

"Izzy—"

"Not here, though. Not like this." He opened his mouth to protest. "Please," she said. He stopped. "You were right. You *are* right. You don't really know how right you are. And I need to tell you. But it can't be here. Meet me tomorrow." Robert shifted, shook his head, and fidgeted with his wedding band again. "No bar this time. Somewhere more appropriate for old friends like us to meet up. Schenley Park? The snow's supposed to let up overnight. It might even be a little warmer tomorrow. Say the ice rink at noon?"

The corner of his mouth turned up. "I haven't been there in I can't remember how long," he said. "I don't know, Izzy."

"Please? I owe you more of an explanation. For so many things." He tilted his head and his forehead creased. "God, I know how cryptic I sound right now, but I promise I will make sense of all of it. Tomorrow."

Robert looked down at his shoes, hands in his pockets. Isabel found herself disarmed by the boyish charm he exuded, even as a distinguished older man, and found it difficult not to embrace him. He looked up from under his brow. "Noon?"

Isabel chewed at the inside of her cheek and nodded.

"See you tomorrow," he said. He backed out the door as she nodded again and turned away so he couldn't see her cover her mouth while the tears fell. She swiped at them when she saw Nico watching her, arms folded. She walked back to her seat at the bar.

"So you're drinking when the brother is paying?" he said. "Who the fuck was that guy?"

Isabel looked back over her shoulder at the door, then back to Nico. "Somebody I realized I wasn't always so nice to," she said.

"Yeah, I know the feeling." He tossed his washrag over his shoulder. The television was tuned to Sports Center again. A mug shot of O.J. flashed on the screen followed by more clips of the trial. Nico shook his finger at the screen and looked back at Isabel. "See?" he said. "You mess with them, you end up dead. Looking like a Pez dispenser." He drew his finger across his neck like a slash.

She opened her mouth to retort but he stormed to the other end of the bar. She sat and stared at the empty glass of club soda in front of her, watched the drops of condensation slide, stop, and slide again, soaking into the cocktail napkin underneath. She looked up to see Nico standing in front of her, his face softened.

"You okay? What did he say to you?"

"Something I needed to hear."

"You going to be all right?"

"Still take you up on that drink?"

He smiled and gave her a heavy pour. He worked his way down the bar, making refills, continuing with his talk about the trial.

Yep, she thought. My dad would have liked you just fine. She finished her drink. Then she had another.

CHAPTER
TEN

obby didn't turn around again. He knew if he did, he'd see Aaron watching him still. *Where the fuck was that bus?* Bobby bounced up and down. He'd surprised himself when he snapped at Aaron. The gun terrified him and he hadn't known what else to do. He had to keep Aaron from hurting someone else. Doing nothing got Bobby here. He would never do nothing again. Still, he couldn't shake the feeling that Aaron had wanted him to stop him. So what, then? Why the show? If he thought he needed to scare Bobby, he hadn't been paying attention. He was already scared out of his mind.

The bus's brakes squealed as it pulled up. The doors opened with a hiss and Bobby flashed the salt-and-pepper-haired black driver his pass. The driver's uniform gave a false semblance of authority and it made Bobby feel better to be near him. Not that he could do anything to help. If Aaron's thick fingers pushed through the folding doors in some gamma radiation-fueled rage, ripped the driver from his seat and threw him into the windshield in some Neo-Nazi frenzy until it spider-webbed and broke loose, there'd be nothing the poor fool would be able to do to stop him. Nor, really, could Bobby. Thankfully, the driver did the only thing he needed to do to avoid all that. He drove off and left Aaron to fade away under the parking lot lights. Tiny rivers of melted snow traveled up and down the channels of the black rubber floor as the bus lurched into gear. The inside lights flickered and dimmed. Bobby sat back and sighed.

The bus was empty except for a man Bobby had been seeing since the beginning of the coldest days of fall. He lay across a section of seats in a dingy gray coat, his face obscured by an overgrown beard, browned the way nicotine stained the filter at the end of Bobby's cigarettes. His pants were stained with who-knew-what, his knit cap full of holes and the heel of one of his work boots peeled away and flopped with each pothole bump. Bobby had never seen him move.

"That guy alive?" Bobby asked the driver

"You want to check for me?" He looked at Bobby in his rearview. Bobby shook his head. The driver chuckled.

"You know his name?" Bobby asked.

"Why you asking?"

Bobby shrugged, though he knew why he asked. Talking to the driver gave his mind something else to do.

"Don't know," the driver said. "He got himself a pass. Catches the first bus in the morning and rides until the last one of the night. Gets off during our breaks, I'm guessing to piss or shit. Cheaper than paying rent and he gets to be warm for a spell."

"He's homeless?"

"Guess so," he said. "I hate to think about somebody with no place to go in this weather. That's why I don't bother him. The other drivers, neither. Could be that he ain't got no home. Could be that he can't go home. Could be he won't. Guys like that always got a story."

Bobby wondered how long the kid Aaron attacked lay there bleeding in the snow with his face crushed before someone found him. What his story was, and if he and Aaron had ended it. He didn't know how he was supposed to live with that, never mind get away with it.

A newspaper sat tucked behind the driver's seat. There had to be something about what happened. Bobby grabbed it.

He scanned the front page. Nothing. Nothing on the inside or on the page after that.

That's impossible.

Nothing in the editorials either. He moved to local news. The front page tore as he whipped past it to get to the inside. Three pages in, he found it. A quarter column in the bottom right-hand corner.

"Student Assaulted Outside Original Hot Dog Shop."

Discovered by his friend shortly after the assault. In stable but critical condition. No eyewitnesses. No suspects. Police reviewing security cameras.

Less than a full paragraph.

Aaron was right. Nobody gave a shit.

Bobby's relief outweighed his guilt and that made him feel worse. Then he read "security cameras" again and his relief jumped ship. He put the paper back behind the driver's seat and leaned his head against the window. It wouldn't take long for them to see something on those video tapes. Maybe he'd be okay, he hadn't gotten out of the truck.

Except he *had* gotten out of the truck.

He'd wanted to stay put, but Aaron convinced him to go in.

How could he have forgotten? His dread wrapped his brain in an opaque film and formed some alternate version of events in an attempt to relieve the crushing culpability.

That's how.

If they saw Aaron, they saw Bobby. Saw him leap into the driver's side while Aaron jumped back in. Saw that same driver's side door not open while a boy lay dying in the street. Saw that same truck speed off without a moment's hesitation, only to slow down a minute later as if nothing happened. Calculated. Saw it slow enough to catch the license plate without even having to freeze the image on the screen. And that would be that. Game over. Just a matter of time. The question was, how much time, and what to do with what's left?

The bus made each light as it cruised down McKnight Road. Bobby tuned into the roar of the engine and was lulled by its constancy. He recalled every moment of the night before, wondering where he could have done something differently to prevent the outcome, until it occurred to him that everything that led to his situation started long ago.

It was the first day of ninth grade. Bobby stood at the white line separating the school bus driver from the rows of faces, most looked nothing like his. The driver yelled at him to take his seat and the kids laughed. He ducked into the empty seat behind the driver and slid down out of sight. The engine rumbled and they drove on.

Bobby pulled an *Avengers* from his backpack and the bus scraped to a stop. The doors opened but he kept his head down. He didn't want to make any more eye contact if he could help it. Someone dropped into the seat next to him: a white kid in a black satin Adidas track jacket and a Pittsburgh Pirates cap cocked to the side. He leaned over Bobby to see what he was reading and Bobby jerked away.

"Marvel comics is wack, yo," the boy said.

Bobby slid over in his seat and pretended to read while the boy reached into his own bag and pulled out a comic, sealed in a plastic bag, but with no white board backing.

What an amateur, Bobby thought.

"Yeah, well," Bobby said, "you should have a board in that if you want it to be worth anything later."

"Please, cuz," the boy said. "Mylar bags is the only way to do it. Can't be using boards unless they acid free." He cocked his head at Bobby's comic. "Probably keep that in one of them long cardboard boxes, huh? Look at it. Pages already getting all yellow and shit."

"No," Bobby said. "I'm not stupid." He closed the comic quickly, not wanting the boy to see where he'd taped the covers inside with scotch tape to keep them from pulling away from the staples. He told himself to throw that long box out when he got home.

"Uh-huh," he said.

"Whatever," Bobby said. "Why are you talking like that?"

"Like what?" he asked.

"You know you're white, right?"

"No, he don't," said a voice behind them. Bobby slid up and looked behind him to see an annoyed black kid. He scrunched up his mouth at Bobby and widened his eyes, gesturing for him to turn around. Bobby held his gaze.

"Was I talking to you?" Bobby said.

"No, but I'm talking to *you*," the kid said.

Bobby turned in his seat when the bus driver shouted for him to face forward. The boy next to him tugged at his shirt and Bobby acquiesced, his eyes on the kid behind until he no longer faced him.

"Anyway," the white kid said. "Y'all tripping."

He opened his bag and slid out an issue of *Crisis on Infinite Earths*, gingerly, as though he was Indiana Jones switching out the idol before the boulder came rolling. Bobby tilted his head to see Superman holding a dead Supergirl in his arms.

"You want to read this one?" he asked and offered his book to him. "DC is where it's at, yo."

"No way, their artists suck," Bobby said.

"What?" He threw his head back. "You *are* tripping! Plus, their stories are way better."

"Come on," Bobby said. "Supergirl? That's like the dumbest character ever."

He looked at the cover and rolled his eyes. "All right, you got that," he said. "She's kind of weak. But they killing her off, so there you go. But she ain't no Ant-Man, I guess, huh? Now that's a dumb-ass character." Bobby laughed in spite of himself and the boy smiled back. "Aaron," he said. He held out his hand.

"Bobby."

Bobby gave him his hand but then Aaron commenced a complicated handshake that Bobby immediately messed up and snatched his hand away.

"You got any more in there?" Bobby asked. Aaron winked and grabbed another *Crisis* issue with The Flash on the cover. "They're killing Flash, too?"

Aaron shrugged, but it was clear he knew the answer. Bobby removed the issue from the sleeve in the same careful manner and Aaron nodded his approval. They read in silence the rest of the way to school.

When the bus pulled up, they stood. The other kids filed by first and wouldn't let them out. Some pushed Aaron as they went by. He looked over his shoulder at Bobby.

"What the hell, man," Bobby said. "Why do you let them do that to you?"

"They just clowning me," he said. "Just playing." His embarrassment was obvious to Bobby, and it made him mad that his new friend got bullied. In some strange way, he was comforted, too, because he no longer felt alone. He wasn't the only one who was different.

They followed the last kid down the steps. Bobby watched them scatter like beans spilled across a table, running and yelling through the front doors of the school. A smile came to his face.

He had a friend. He almost had to say it out loud to believe it.

Sure, he was a little weird, but he liked comics and he liked Bobby. He saw that although he wasn't looking at him, Aaron was smiling, too.

Aaron walked with Bobby to the office to help him find his homeroom and later showed him where some of his classes were. They didn't have any of the same ones; Aaron said his classes were exceptional, but then he got that same look on his face as when the kids pushed him on the bus, so Bobby didn't ask what it meant. Aaron brightened when he saw that they had lunch at the same time and they agreed to meet up then.

Bobby stood at the entrance to the cafeteria but he couldn't find Aaron and started to panic. He tried not to see the all the glares and stares as he looked through the crowd for him. No one seemed to want him there. Not the few tables where the white kids congregated and not the black kids, either. He found himself in the center of the cafeteria, turning in every direction, looking for a seat, looking for Aaron, and finding neither. He told himself he wasn't that hungry, which was quickly becoming the truth, and turned to leave. He'd eat at home, save the lunch he packed for tomorrow.

Where is Aaron? Why the hell is everyone looking at me?

The noise of the cafeteria swelled and Bobby found it harder to breathe. Someone grabbed his arm from behind and his heart climbed into his throat before it dove into his stomach. He pulled his arm away, dropped his lunch, and cocked his fist.

"Get off me!"

Bobby's shout echoed and the din hushed. He turned to see Aaron and his cheeks tingled and his ears burned. The cafeteria burst into laughter, and Bobby waited for Aaron to do the same.

But he didn't. He put his arm around Bobby and guided him to two empty chairs at the end of a long table. When they sat, the kids that sat there got up and moved a few seats down. Aaron seemed not to notice. He pulled a bagged lunch from his backpack along with two other comics. He slid one over to Bobby. His heart slowed and his appetite returned. They read and ate while the rest of the world ignored them. That was just fine with Bobby.

Aaron's talk and dress made him an outcast to just about everyone. The black kids were insulted by his impersonation of them, which even Bobby thought was pretty terrible, and it caught him no end of bullying, with Bobby guilty by association, though they dished it out less when Bobby was around. The white kids wanted to avoid the same trouble and treated them like the untouchables in India that they read about in their social studies class.

Bobby almost admired how much he committed to it, though. It wasn't for show. He didn't drop the act when they were alone. He didn't straighten his hat or listen to different music. He was genuinely confused as to why the black kids he wanted to be like constantly dismissed him. The way they treated him for it turned Bobby's fear of them into disgust, and he pushed the truth about his father down so deep that he no longer believed it. He hated the truth, and that truth made him hate them, which resulted in more than one trip to the principal's office for scuffles in the hall, standing up for Aaron when he couldn't, or wouldn't do it for himself.

Aaron wanted to be like them no matter how much Bobby told him he was embarrassing himself. How he should have some self-respect. He thought about what his grandfather would say if he knew he hung out with someone like Aaron, and wondered at times if he shouldn't. But he and Aaron were misfits, each in their own way.

They spent every lunch together. They walked the halls and

ignored the taunts of their label, the Comic Book Queers. They always finished their food before the end of lunch and sat outside and read under a breezeway.

Aaron joked one day with Bobby that they should kiss and really freak everyone out. Bobby remembered Grandpap's tirades about poofs and fags, about how they were spreading some virus and undermining society—and he'd heard it enough to believe it himself. Aaron laughed, but there was an uneasiness about it. It made Bobby angry.

"That's not funny, man."

"Oh, come on," Aaron said, "You don't got a sense of humor about *anything*."

"Queers are disgusting," Bobby spit back. "Don't even joke about that. Seriously,"

Aaron laughed again, told Bobby to relax, and went back to his comic. He didn't talk for the rest of lunch and he never mentioned it again.

Later that same day, Bobby found Aaron on the floor in the restroom with a bloody nose and a split lip. His eyes were wet and swollen. Bobby helped him up and gave him a wet paper towel. Aaron hissed in pain as he pressed it to his lip.

"What happened this time?" Bobby asked.

"Nothing," he said.

"Why do you keep trying to be like them when this is what you get? I keep telling you, they're animals. My Grandpap tried to tell me and I didn't listen. You need to listen to me."

Aaron shoved Bobby backwards. "Would you leave me alone? I never even said who it was that did it, did I?" Bobby stood with his back to the wall, open-mouthed. "God," Aaron said. "I'm going to class. See you later, I guess."

Aaron was right. Bobby had assumed it was the black kids again.

He stewed with a confused mix of frustration and sympathy for Aaron. He wanted to tell him right then about his father, because despite their inseparable nature, there stood this divide between them, and at that moment, Aaron seemed more alone than ever. But he knew it would hurt Aaron to know that in some sense, he had what Aaron wanted, to not just be like them but to *be* them, and that Bobby wanted no part of it would be like throwing it in Aaron's face, He thought Aaron might even resent him for it. He couldn't lose his only friend. He also knew, out of some innate sense of self-preservation, that to the black kids with whom he fought to protect Aaron, the revelation about who he really was might bring him more harm than good. Bobby didn't tell Aaron then and he promised himself he never would.

He would never tell anyone.

The oversized wipers squealed across the windshield as the bus passed through Shadyside and drew closer to Homewood. A scant few passengers got on and off in-between. They probably went home to a comfortable boredom, to the same old job with the same old people, taking for granted the lack of anxiety of it all. Bobby could say "hello" and they'd forget him as soon as they stepped off the bus.

But maybe not.

Maybe they'd find out they had something common, the way he and Aaron did that first day of school. Maybe their lives would be changed forever. Maybe for the better, but probably for the worse, because everything falls apart. It has to.

There was a lecture in sophomore chemistry that always stuck with Bobby. It was about entropy, this idea that the natural order of the world skewed towards disorder. He'd had a hard time with the concept until the teacher put it a way he understood. Your room doesn't get cleaner, it gets messier, she'd said. It's the same with the universe. He became obsessed with the idea. He started sketching a villain in his notebook. The villain was a mutant, born to a drug-abusing mother whose only ability was to bring chaos to the lives of anyone with whom he came in physical contact. Bobby named him Entropy. When he showed him to Aaron, he'd been dismayed to learn that was already a character in the Marvel universe. Then Bobby picked up a thesaurus and went with Bedlam. Same problem. Aaron said it was a stupid character anyway and Bobby eventually scrapped it.

Bobby laughed to himself. He hadn't thought about that in years.

The bus took a tight corner and hit a curb. The bump shook the homeless rider and he stirred but didn't wake. What put you here, Bobby thought. Was it your choices, or were you just another result of entropy? A victim of circumstance who deserved pity, or a criminal, maybe even a murderer who was lucky to be sleeping on a bus? He might not know if he'd eat the next day or if he'd get rolled for the change he scraped together by someone just a little more desperate than he. But as long as he had money for the bus, he knew where he'd be tomorrow. He knew that his future was, in some ways, predictable. Though Bobby never knew if he and his mother would make rent from month to month, there was certainty in the fact that they'd work more than they played, that they lived shift-to-shift, and there would be nights where he'd sweep up the debris of her broken promises. As shitty as it was, there was comfort in their routine. He wanted that feeling back and he realized there was only one way to get it.

The bus turned onto Frankstown Avenue. Bobby reached to pull the cord to ring the bell, then stopped. "How much longer you on?" he asked the driver.

"Couple more hours," the driver said. "Why?"

"Mind if I go around again?"

He looked up at Bobby in the rearview, shrugged and nodded.

"What's your story?" he asked.

"Still writing it," Bobby said. He drove on. Bobby recalled his Entropy character again. He should have named him Aaron.

CHAPTER
ELEVEN

The bus ran its full route again and roared down Frankstown for a second time. Bobby pulled the cord. The bus came to a stop at the corner of the block and Bobby made his way down the steps.

"Go easy, young man," the driver said.

Bobby turned back. The sincerity in the driver's voice and the warmth of his smile made Bobby feel safe. He could go around for one more loop, but the reflective sanctuary of the bus was only temporary. He'd made his mind up what he needed to do and the longer he waited, the less likely he was do it. He nodded his head at the driver and he returned the gesture. The doors hissed shut and the engine growled until the brake lights winked out of view. Bobby raised his hand in a wave, already somehow missing both him and his homeless companion who would sleep until the sun came up, or until a less gracious driver kicked him off. His sanctuary gone, Bobby's anxiety took firm hold again and he hurried down the half block to the apartment. The Fox was parked out front and had a light dusting of snow on the hood. It hadn't been there long. He'd hoped Mom had stayed for an overnight shift, but if he was lucky, she'd be asleep. He still needed time to figure out how to tell her what had happened, his plan, everything. But he was exhausted. Just a few hours of sleep. Then he'd let her know what he had done.

He shoved the key in and the door opened with a gentle push. It was already unlocked. The apartment smelled of Drakkar and cigarettes. A throaty snore reverberated from down the hall, too deep even for Isabel.

Unbelievable.

Every time she rode the wagon away from the bar, it was if she sat in precarious balance on the edge of it, inches away from falling off when it struck a rut in the road, and that son-of-a-bitch Nico enabled her every step of the way back to that shit watering hole. Bobby wished he had the stones to kick open the door and yoke him by his midget neck, throw him out in the hall and lock the door behind him, leaving him with his clothes wadded up in his arms, shivering. But Bobby knew that was all fantasy. He was no more a tough guy than Nico. He wished he had been. Maybe he wouldn't have ended up in this spot.

The couch never looked so comfortable and Bobby face-planted onto it. While the bus ran its loop, his mind did, too. He had to call the cops and turn them both in. He would tell them Aaron threatened him and that he had no choice but to drive away or he'd kill him. He hadn't had a gun then, but he had one in the glove compartment now. Maybe when they came to get them, that would seem like a reasonable story and they'd go easy on Bobby, maybe even let him go. But if they'd reviewed the tapes, it would already be too late. Any story he'd give them now would sound like covering his own ass. And what if Aaron somehow got off on claiming self-defense or some other bullshit. Then what? Would he come after Bobby?

Before that night, the idea that Aaron would do anything of the sort was like an issue of *What If...?* where Uatu the Watcher narrated the alternate realities of the Marvel Universe. In this issue, Bobby's best friend has become a Neo-Nazi psycho killer. If Bobby had just said *"fuck the Original, their pizza blows,"* they would have hit the Taco Bell drive-thru and eaten their faces off. Aaron would have drunk himself stupid. The next morning they would catch up on all the things he'd missed while he was locked up. They'd freak out about all the good artists leaving Marvel and starting Image. How Keaton rocked it as Batman the second time and how they turned the Ninja Turtles into a fucking kid's franchise even though Raphael was still kind of badass. Somewhere in the middle of all that, Bobby would have helped him forget what happened to him inside, back to some semblance of normal.

But that was the real *What If...?* *That* was the alternate reality.

Aaron deserved to go back to jail. But isn't jail what did this to him? They tore out his hair and knocked out his teeth. Fucked his face and raped him.

God, what would they do to me? *Where would I sit in* that *cafeteria?*

As small as the apartment was, as much he hated that couch and despised their slumlord, he was no warden, the couch no metal bunk. The rooms had doors, and those doors had locks that Bobby controlled, and he shit and showered in private.

The idea of turning Aaron in lost steam.

So run. As far and as fast as you can. You can wait tables anywhere. You don't own a cell phone, no credit card. Even if they see your face on those tapes, the truck's not registered to you. You're as good as gone. A ghost. Even if they pulled in Aaron, he'd never turn you in.

He'd never turn you in.

He'd never turn you in.

As Bobby faded from the fatigue, his brain conjured living comic book panels. Aaron was a steroid-pumped Red Skull knock-off, sieg-heiling and goose-stepping, while Bobby was the Peter Parker nerd but without the super powers, still fighting to keep his true identity a secret from the evil super villain. They engaged in an epic battle of wits versus brawn as he drifted off to sleep.

He woke up hours later in the middle of an asthma attack. He'd had one of those dreams where he fought a faceless someone, but every punch he threw was in slow motion, like pushing his limbs through peanut butter. His punches barely found the mark, and when they did, they had no effect on his anonymous opponent. So he ran. That didn't work, either. No matter how loud his brain yelled at his legs to advance, they stayed stuck in a different time, pulling and pushing against some invisible force. Then the dream changed. Now he fell through ice, his mouth filled with freezing water, dirty and putrid, until he vomited. That's when he woke up face down on a drool-covered cushion and gasping for air. He grasped in his pocket and sucked on his inhaler until the boa constrictor let go of his chest.

Down the hall, Isabel's door creaked open. Whispers drifted out soon after. Bobby heard Nico tell Isabel that he thought Bobby looked asleep. He kept his head leaned back against the couch, his eyes only open a slit and faked a snore for good measure. The hinges squealed as the door opened fully and Bobby strained to listen for footsteps on the threadbare carpet that covered the cold slab. Then, underneath his eyelids, he saw movement, smelled Nico's cologne. Nico took long soft steps, Elmer Fudd stalking Bugs in hunting season. Bobby held back a laugh. Nico watched him with each careful step, and when Bobby opened his eyes and lifted his head, he cursed under his breath.

"Hey, Bobby."

"Hey, asshole."

"Right. Good to see you again, Bobby. Nice talking to you." He zipped his coat to his chin and made for the door.

"Stay away from my mother, jagoff," Bobby shouted after him. He shook his head and caught a glimpse of Isabel standing in the doorway. She wore a tattered terry bathrobe of the most horrendous periwinkle that Bobby had bought for her many Christmases ago with money he'd saved from his earliest jobs. He insisted she throw it away, but she never did.

"That's not what it looked like," she said. "Not exactly. He drove me home and fell asleep making sure I was okay."

"Oh, well then that's much better," Bobby said, throwing his hands up. "Two days in a row, Mom? Jesus Christ. No falling off the wagon for you. You just jump."

She tucked her hand into the worn pockets and walked down the hall, head bowed, hair pulled back. She sat next to him on the couch and put her hand on his knee. "Can you let me explain?"

Bobby put his face in his hands and leaned back again, talking into them. "Is it going to be anything different than the usual? I can't keep doing this, Mom."

"I know," she said.

"I don't think you do," he said. "I mean I literally can't do this anymore. You have to find a way to do this yourself."

"I'm trying."

"Try harder!"

Isabel jumped at his shout and pulled her hand away from his knee. She pinched the lapels of her robe closer together. "Bobby, what's going on with you?"

"Nothing." He laughed. "Everything. Whatever. It doesn't fucking matter. What time is it? I should see if I can pick up a lunch shift since you're in no condition."

"I didn't get drunk last night. I mean, not like normal. Nico just didn't think I should drive."

"See, that sentence should have been 'I didn't *drink* last night,' Mom. See the difference?"

"You're right. I know you're right."

"All right, so why? Why even *one* drink at that sleaze bag's bar?"

Isabel inhaled deeply, then let out a stuttered breath. "I asked you yesterday if you trust me. Do you remember?"

"Yeah."

"If I try to explain to you what's happened over the last two days, you won't let me get past the first situation, and I wouldn't blame you. It *will* sound like all the same old bullshit. Up until a point, it was. But if you really do trust me, then I need you to go somewhere with me. It's not far, but you can't ask me any questions until we get there. If you do that, I can promise you that I will *never* have another drink. I'll go to meetings if that's what it takes. I'd swear on something but we don't really have anything worth a damn except you, so, you know, there's that."

They shared a genuine but tired laugh. Bobby opened his mouth to tell her no, that he needed to make sure they made rent this month, but then he remembered the billfold of hundreds in his back pocket. He planned to find Aaron's bag in the back, get his keys and somehow get to his truck unnoticed and put it back in the glove compartment, disgusted with himself that he ever took it in the first place, but if he ended up in jail, it would sit in some evidence locker while his mother might end up on the street. Isabel looked at him with a conviction he'd always wished for when she promised these things before. He didn't trust her then, but something in her voice, something in her eyes made him trust her now.

"All right," he said. "I'll go."

Isabel slapped his knee and beamed. "All right. You want a shower?"

"Go ahead." He yawned. "I'm still waking up."

Isabel sprung from the couch and nearly bounded down the hall. When Bobby was sure she was in the shower, he went to the mason jar above the kitchen sink. He fanned out the billfold and stared at it for a minute. He counted out enough for next month's rent and stashed the rest in his pocket, resolved to put it back.

He could live with that.

CHAPTER TWELVE

Isabel couldn't help but look at Bobby at every stop sign, every traffic light. God, he looked nothing like Robert and yet so much like him, especially now. They'd see the resemblance in each other's faces instantly. She just knew it. Bobby smiled each time he caught her staring, but she saw his annoyance growing, in that harmless way sons get annoyed with their mothers when they treat their grown young men like the little boys they still are to them.

"What?" he asked.

"When did you get so handsome?"

"What's gotten into you?" He rolled down the window a crack. "The cap fall off your body spray?"

He was right. She'd gone overboard. She kept it in check with the wardrobe, though. Tasteful. She wore a smart button-down with only the top two left undone and black slacks with a sharp crease past the knee. She let her hair down, swept to one side. The makeup was solid, too, not too much, not too little. It wasn't for Robert, though. This was a day she would never forget, one way or the other. Whether for a wedding or a funeral, people always dressed their best.

"We agreed, no questions," she said. "That was two."

Bobby held his hands up and looked out his window. She missed this, the affectionate snarky exchanges between them. She missed that smile. It looked so real she almost didn't believe it. A horn sounded as she ignored a four-way stop. She stopped the car short of being clipped and Bobby braced himself on the dash.

"Jesus, Mom."

She apologized. Her heart thrummed, already at a breakneck pace with the anticipation of what waited for them in a few short miles. She felt that same feeling twenty-two years ago, driving to deliver the exact same revelation to Robert. She hoped this day would end much differently than that one had.

She hadn't thought anything of throwing up the morning she found out. At least not at first. She'd been out late the night before and lost count of the shots, although she remembered the number for the taxi. Hangover sick felt different. *This* was different. It couldn't have been what she knew it probably was, but it made scary sense.

They both hated condoms.

"I want to feel you," he'd said.

She told him she did, too, and she really did. He pulled out in time, he had to have, she was sure, but maybe not *so* sure, so she sprinted to the bathroom and peed it out. It was just once and she thought she got it all out. What were the chances? How fertile could she be? Had enough time even passed? She counted the days in her head and when she came up with the number she fought the urge to vomit again.

She couldn't look at food that morning. Even her morning cigarette made her so nauseous she tossed it after one drag, and forget about the hair of the dog. Stomach flu, that had to be it. When she could no longer convince herself, it was off to the free clinic.

She couldn't hear anything the doctor said after he told her. The sound of his voice dulled, her head in a diver's helmet. She felt weightless and heavy all at once, like she'd float away, but the nervous sweat on the backs of her thighs stuck her to the exam table.

I can't take care of a kid. I can barely take care of myself.

That some child would be screaming every night and depending on her to keep it alive, let alone love it, seemed a like a cruel joke that she wasn't in on.

Still, something stirred in her that she couldn't deny. In between the dramatic swings of complete terror and familiar self-loathing floated this tiny atom of joy. This feeling that God had made all as it should be and that this was her test. Her way to straighten out. A child would force her to dry out and to get clear.

Maybe Mama could watch the kid during the day and I could get a real job, maybe finish up those credits so I could be something, maybe even a role model for this kid.

For instants of time as tiny as that new life inside of her, Isabel felt happy.

But she liked her life. Liked that she answered to no one. The only appeal school held for her rested in the parties and when she discovered she could enjoy them without the burden of classes, she found a job waiting tables on campus, a roommate in one of the waitresses at the diner, and dropped out to carefree days and quick money. The idea of "adult" responsibility petrified her, but then, she didn't have to do this alone. Until she realized she did.

She found him in the game room at the student union. When she reached for the door, she saw him. And *her*. Short shorts revealed long legs of deep brown skin, darker than Robert by far. She leaned on his shoulder while he chalked the tip of his cue. Her hand trailed down his back as he bent over the table to take his shot, her eyes travelling down the length of his legs, until they looked up to meet Isabel's, staring from the doorway. Isabel stepped to the side, flattening herself up against wall next to the glass double-doored entrance.

Tell him you're pregnant and he'll be with you. He'll have to be. But he'll resent you forever.

Resent you? Who is he to resent you? He's in there with another girl and didn't even have the nerve to tell you to your face. He's no father, and you can't do this on your own. That's no life for a child.

She stood up straight, another wave of nausea cresting.

You know what you need to do. What you have to do.

Her eyes burned. She ran for the exit with her hand over her mouth and pushed through the doors to the outside. The sky had yellowed. Muscular clouds rolled over each other. Lightning flashes lit their billows and the quiet thunder rumbled like a slow rolling bowling ball. Another wave of nausea and she swallowed back hot bile. A drink didn't sound so bad anymore and a smoke sounded even better. She lit up from a smashed pack in her back pocket and took a nice long drag. She knew where she had to go next, so what did it matter?

She parked the car outside of the clinic and kept it running. A coffee stained napkin stuck to the inside of a cup holder next to the steering wheel and she pulled it away. Some of it stayed stuck to the plastic. She tore it obsessively into browned confetti that littered her legs. Fat drops of rain thumped the windshield before a downpour washed the pollen from the windows in yellowish-green streaks and beat the car roof so loudly it almost drowned out the radio. She turned it up, heard Croce's "Time in A Bottle", and turned it right off.

She unlatched her seatbelt, untucked her tank top and pulled it up over her stomach, pushing out her hollowed belly. A little mound formed and she traced circles on it with her index finger.

She sat up and pulled down her shirt.

The drops hit hard as hail. Isabel drummed her fingers on the steering wheel in time. The cracks of thunder were the only thing louder than the rain.

It wouldn't be fair to keep it. Boys need a father

Oh, a father like yours? Would that be fair? You can do this better than he did.

In the passenger seat, three fifths of vodka sat in paper bags. Isabel'd bought them before she went to find Robert. She hoped to get drunk with him one last time and fall into bed with him where he'd kiss her stomach before moving further down. She pinched her arm hard so the memory of how good he could make her feel would be replaced with pain, like the slap in the face of seeing him with that girl's arm lingering on his back, where Isabel's hand once rested. Where it belonged. She laughed, then cried, then screamed. Who was she kidding? What a fucking mess. She couldn't be a mother to a son.

A son. That was the second time she thought of the baby as a "him." She didn't know why. She just *knew*. With that, her reasons not to keep him didn't matter anymore, because there was no little atom anymore, there was a "him." She smiled and giggled and couldn't stop doing either.

She put the car in drive and pulled away from the clinic.

On the drive home, though, her mind changed in time with the traffic lights.

Green. This is the best thing ever, he's a gift.

Yellow. But maybe not now. Maybe now that you know you really want a baby, you should wait until you get a little more stable. Don't keep this one. You don't really know it's a "him." Hell, you might only want him because you think deep down you can still get Robert to stay with you. Jesus, settle down, girl, and think a little bit.

Red. You are out of your fucking mind. Call Robert. He doesn't want a baby and neither do you. Maybe he'll even pay for the procedure. Get rid of this thing and live the life you enjoy. You want to be up all night? You want to give up partying? Can you? Get real.

She hit a number of red lights on the way home.

Isabel and her mother cleared plates from dinner when her water broke. A dish hit the tile and shattered, sending ceramic slivers across the floor. Her mother started the breathing exercises while she set the kitchen timer for the contractions. Isabel watched a crescent-shaped shard rock back and forth on its curve like a bassinet. Her father yelled from the living room and broke the trance.

Isabel grabbed her belly and pleaded for the baby to stop knifing her from the inside while she stood in a puddle of herself.

Just give me one more week, because I'm not ready, not now.

She realized then that she wasn't ever going to be ready because it wasn't just the baby coming. Now came sleepless nights, a sagging stomach, and someone else's everything to clean up. She had to love it, love him, more than herself and she didn't know that she could. She leaned against the counter and leaked on her parents' linoleum while she mimicked her mother's breathing, less to control the pain, because it didn't, but to keep from having a panic attack. It failed at that as well.

Her father parked the car while her mother wheeled Isabel into the emergency entrance. A nurse took the hand-off and rolled her back to Labor and Delivery, wincing at Isabel's shrieks for an epidural. Every contraction felt like a tidal wave, rising and smashing down into her stomach. She threw up all over herself. She wanted to take the face of every customer at the diner where she worked who told her how lucky she was, how beautiful childbirth could be, and shove it through a plate glass window. Why hadn't she gone into the clinic and taken the next available appointment? Whatever it would have taken to keep her out of this moment, as this baby pulled her apart from the inside. She didn't want this anymore.

It was too late for the epidural. They wheeled her bed into the delivery room and placed her heels in the cold steel stirrups. In between contractions she thought about the ruin this baby would make of her body and how no man would ever want her again. Pain spiked and she screamed for them to get him out of her. She started to hyperventilate with panic.

How do I get out of this? Who can I leave him with? Who could I convince to take care of him?

They said push, and she pushed, and she smelled shit and started crying.

It's crowning, the doctor said, in a voice as excited as she knew she should have been.

When he told her it was a boy, all her doubts went away in a breath, a candle extinguished. She inhaled and it didn't hurt, not like before. A calm, almost alarming in its immediacy, overtook her, and in that moment, she took it all back, everything terrible thing she'd thought.

She asked to hold him, but the doctor turned his back to her and walked the baby to a table. Two nurses huddled around him and another nurse came to Isabel's side and took her hand. It was so quiet. The nurse's breathing rasped loud through her mask.

"Why isn't he crying?" Isabel asked.

The nurse stroked her hair.

Then it wasn't quiet. Isabel heard wet sucking sounds like the plastic hook they used at the dentist's office and there was still no crying.

"Is something wrong?" Isabel asked.

The nurse gripped her hand tighter and Isabel's tears fell unbidden. She regretted every drink she told herself she shouldn't have, every cigarette she promised was the last, every late night. She just wanted to hear him cry. The doctor murmured and one of the nurses left his side to pick up a phone in the room. The sucking sound continued and the nurse pulled down her mask to speak into the receiver.

Then he mewled like a kitten. Her nurse's cheeks rose up over the border of her mask and turned her eyes to slits. She sandwiched Isabel's hand between hers and rubbed the back of it. The warmth of it spread up her arm and into her chest. The doctor turned from the table with her little man swaddled and resting on his forearm. He could have fit in one of the doctor's hands. The doctor held him out to her, and though she'd never held a baby, her arms knew what to do. His little red wrinkly face looked mushed and bruised. He had a nest of straight black hair and Isabel let out a breath of relief that, at least for the moment, he didn't look like his father, at least not in the ways that would matter to her father. He yawned big and made little pig snorts and his tiny hands opened and closed. Isabel couldn't stop giggling.

"He's beautiful," said the nurse.

"Oh, God, no, he's not." Isabel smiled. "But you have to say that." The nurse batted her shoulder. "He's ugly, but he's mine." The nurse who picked up the phone came towards Isabel and reached for the baby.

Isabel pulled away. She told her no.

The doctor stood from his table and another nurse joined him. Isabel held him closer. Why did they want to take him from her? Isabel looked up to her nurse and pleaded for her not to let them. The doctor stood next to her and said they needed to take him to the nursery for additional measurements and that he'd ordered a respiratory consult because of all the fluid they'd had to suction. His snorting and his weak cries and his weight and his breathing all were reason for concern. Isabel didn't want to let him go but her nurse had kind eyes. She trusted her when she held out her arms for him.

"Don't you worry. He'll be in good hands," she said. "And then he'll be in yours."

His tiny neck muscles flexed with each small breath, and he whistled when he inhaled. He struggled for air. Isabel swore she'd throw out her cigarettes. When she looked into the eyes of her doctors and nurses, no judgment resided there. She cradled him in her hands and handed him to her nurse. She thanked Isabel and handed him to another nurse who put him in a rolling bin and wheeled him out the double doors.

"Did you pick a name?" she asked.

The doors swung shut and she ached to see him again, an ache so similar to when she realized Robert was gone. But her child wouldn't leave her. He would come back. He would love her forever.

"Bobby," Isabel said. She laid back and closed her eyes, and fell asleep before she reached her room.

The dash clock read ten past noon when they pulled in to the far end of the parking lot next to the Schenley Park ice rink. Isabel checked her face in the mirror and saw Bobby watching her from the corner of her eye. She pulled her hair back, then let it down, then pulled it back again. She turned to Bobby who continued to gaze at her in confusion.

"What?" she asked.

"You tell me. What are you doing?"

"Just a few more minutes, hon, I swear."

The rink overflowed with parents and kids who took advantage of the snow day. Isabel scanned the crowds until she found him. He wore heather gray slacks with a razor crease and a black pea coat. Damn him, he looked good. He leaned on the outside wall of the rink. A father and his young daughter held hands and half-walked, half-skated around the edge. The girl guided her father instead of the other way around. When they rounded the turn and got closer to Robert, the dad lost his balance, eyes wide, feet skittering, and clutched for the wall. Robert shot out his hand to help while the little girl grabbed her daddy by the forearm. She laughed, but not at him. So proud to be his rescuer. Robert smiled at them as they skated off and Isabel watched him watch them. She saw that same sadness from the night before. This was her chance. She turned and stopped in front of Bobby.

"I need you to wait here," she said. She pointed to a bench next to them.

"Seriously, Mom, what is this? I've never been on a pair of skates and I'm not in the mood to learn today. Really, I got to get in to the bistro and see if I can get a closing shift."

"Just. Sit."

He breathed out in a huff and sat. Isabel brought her hands to her mouth in a prayer position.

"Thank you. Ten minutes. Just give me ten minutes. I'll be right back." Bobby nodded his assent, leaned back, and spread his arms across the back of the bench. Isabel backed away a few feet, then turned to walk towards Robert.

He turned to see her and smiled. Not a big smile, but warm, almost relieved. Her feet and lips felt like they went numb. She wondered if it was possible to scare herself into a stroke, because as soon as he saw her, she felt pure terror. She hadn't thought this through. Somehow, she had it in her mind that she'd shake his hand, talk about the weather and tell him about his grown son.

Did I mention he thinks you're dead because I told him so. Because you broke my heart? I mean, yeah, you're right, it was my fault, but I didn't know that at the time, so uh, whoops. By the way, I named him after you since it was the only way to have you around. That's not weird, is it?

Oh, my God, this is the stupidest thing I've ever done.

He walked towards her. She wiped her hand on her pants and stuck it out for a shake at the same time he lifted his arms. *Jesus, is he going to hug me, what the hell am I supposed to do with that?* She quickly switched to open arms and he switched to one hand to meet her handshake at the same time and they froze in those positions and laughed. It felt good, a small measure of relief. Then he really hugged her. Tears welled and she willed them back. She wrapped her arms around his waist, put her head against his chest and inhaled. She realized he had stopped and that she still held on so she gave him three hard slaps to the back and let him go.

"I thought you might have forgotten," he said.

"Sorry," she said. "I had a thing at a place." He smirked. "No, I didn't. Sorry I'm late." She tilted her head towards the rink. "Want to lace 'em up?"

"Brothers weren't made for the ice," he said. "Besides, falling is bad for my ego."

"Thank God," she said. "If you said yes, I was screwed."

He laughed again.

"Want to walk, then?" she said.

"Yeah, that sounds good."

Isabel wanted him to offer the crook of his arm so she could lace her arms through and around it, so she could rest her head on his shoulder as they strolled through the park. Despite the warmth of his greeting, despite the laughs just now, she knew that time was lost to them. She reminded herself, for the final time, that this was not her time. He put his hands in his pockets and she did the same. She swallowed around the tennis ball in her throat and they moved away from the rink and onto the walking path, taking them into the park and towards Bobby. Then Robert's pager went off.

CHAPTER
THIRTEEN

When Robert awoke that morning, he almost cancelled the whole thing. Had he thought to get Isabel's phone number, he would have. It wasn't about old feelings resurfacing, at least not the ones he needed to be concerned about in that way. It hurt to see her again. To remember the fear he felt of their relationship being discovered. About what her father would do. How hard he worked to not be afraid, and how badly he wanted Isabel to understand that it was no game. How much he wanted to stop caring about her, to make it easy to walk away. That even though it seemed to her that it was, it wasn't. He didn't want to remember what that felt like. He wanted to be as angry at her as she clearly had been with him all these years, and yet didn't want to give her the satisfaction of his anger.

Still, he told her. He said everything he'd wanted to say so many years ago. It surprised him, the weight those emotions still placed on him, decades old. He didn't think it possible for it to still matter. It wasn't in the instant that he recognized who she was that he realized it, but in the moment he told her what she'd meant to him. What her dismissal of his fear, conscious or not, meant to him. Why it caused his response to her injury to him was to be hurt back. It lifted the load. Set it aside. The feeling almost euphoric, too good not to share.

Showered and dressed, he walked down the steps and stood in front of the French doors to the dining room. The divorce filings sat in wait, no wishing enough to vanish them from the table. He pulled open the doors and sat. He tapped his fingers on the edge of the papers, flattening them at the crease, until he picked up the pen next to them. He dragged the documents towards him, hunched over them, and signed.

Pages flipped, signatures scrawled, he left the dining room, walked to his home office, and faxed the paperwork to Tamara's attorney. A different lightness sat in his chest as the pages fed through the machine. When finished, he folded the papers and walked to the fire safe in the office closet. An empty folder sat just in front of one that contained their medical records. Records that included the report from the final visit to the obstetrician. Robert filed them and closed the safe.

"I'm sorry," he said.

He walked towards the front of the house. Isabel opened a door, offered a chance to close another, and he needed to walk through.

The main lot at Schenley Park was crowded for a weekday. The snow from the night before had been cleared and the bright afternoon sun melted the snow banks despite the chill in the air. Steam rose from the damp pavement. Robert shielded his eyes from the snow glare and looked around the half-full lot. He saw no sign of Isabel so he walked down the path leading to the ice rink.

A young girl ran past him, chased by her brother, giggling furiously. It made him miss Tamara instantly. She had a giggle like that; when he spooned her and tickled her belly when they found out they were pregnant. He remembered the way she'd reach behind her and pull his face into her neck. He'd nuzzle in and run his hand over the lower part of her stomach and feel for the bump to come. She'd guide his hand down further and slide his finger into her with a gasp. They'd lie in the middle of the bed, pressed against each other as hard as they could. He never imagined that the middle of their bed would become a dividing line that neither of them would cross again. Signing those papers had been a mistake.

Snow bowed the branches of the trees that lined the walkway and coated them like icing. The high afternoon sun poked through openings of the jagged canopy. The melting snow fell like rain on the asphalt footpath. A bough loosed its sleeve of snow and it hit the ground with a wet smack. The limb bobbed as if it was waving. It either beckoned him forward or warned him away. Robert walked on.

Shrieks of children's laughter echoed in the air as he approached the rink. The roads had still been covered in some areas and the radio said the threat of another round of the storm changed the school delays to cancellations. Parents played hooky from work with their children. Some kids skated with a practiced fluidity while their parents trailed behind them, their faces aglow with pride. Others flailed like newborn colts testing their legs as the blades of their skates chopped at the ice. Mothers and fathers followed behind with their arms outstretched and ready to catch them when they fell. Robert leaned his elbows on the wall of the rink and watched.

A hand grabbed the rail of the rink in front of Robert with a slap. The man it belonged to pulled himself up from a near fall on the ice.

A girl who appeared to be his daughter, no older than ten, slid to a stop at his side. He pushed himself up with her help while his skates slid back and forth in a dramatic attempt to gain his footing, all for the benefit of his little girl. He winked at Robert. She twittered, and he and Robert shared a knowing smile. He thanked his daughter over and over for helping him and they joined the rest of the skaters on the outer circle.

Robert checked his watch. It seemed Isabel wasn't coming, and he felt no small amount of relief. When he turned back towards the walking path, he saw her. She smiled and waved. When they reached each other, she extended her hand at the same time he opened his arms for an embrace. He offered his hand and she opened her arms until they both settled on a hug. It was a good one. He smelled a man's cologne and the sour smell of alcohol coming from her skin. She gave an extra squeeze along with a few hard pats and pulled away.

They walked. She glanced back and forth from her shoes to him, her face tight with the anticipation of something to say. Just when she looked ready to say it, his pager beeped. He looked down and his eyes widened when he saw a California exchange. He looked around for a pay phone and found one just behind them.

"I'm so sorry," he said. "Give me just one minute. I'll be right back." He didn't wait for Isabel's reaction and quick stepped to the phone. She picked up on the first ring.

"That was fast," Tamara said.

"I mean, yeah, you know." Robert said. "It's not like. I wasn't waiting. I just..." He rolled his eyes and shook his head at his clumsiness. He looked down the path at Isabel. She looked away, caught staring, and shifted back and forth, one foot to the other. Her nervousness distracted him for a moment.

"Thank you," she said.

Robert snapped to. "I'm sorry," he said. "For what?"

Tamara stayed silent.

"Oh, yes," he said. "Of course."

Neither of them spoke. Tamara's breath paused, then resumed. Robert envisioned her chin dropping to let the words, any words come, dying in her open mouth. Each time he went to speak, those little pauses came, and so he refrained, until she broke the silence.

"Take care of yourself, Robert," she said.

A protest rose. *Let's stay in touch. A call here and there. Maybe dinner when you're back in town.*

He knew what her words meant. His dissent receded.

"You, too, Tamara. For what it's worth, I'm sorry."

She let out a sigh. "It's worth a lot." Another breath. "Bye." A click and the line went silent.

Early in their relationship, when Tamara traveled for conferences, they'd stay on the phone well into the night. One made the other commit to hanging up first, though only the one who called could disconnect the call. If the other hung up first, the call would reconnect if the other side lifted the receiver again. They'd battle back and forth until one finally gave in, succumbing to fatigue and the threat of endless hours of work the following morning.

Robert and listened for Tamara to pick up. Then he replaced the receiver in the cradle.

He turned back to Isabel who greeted him with another smile as he walked back towards her.

"Everything okay?" she asked.

"Yes," he said. "And no. But yes."

"Okay. That's good. I guess?"

"Isabel," he said. "I have to go."

"Wait. What? What did I say?"

"Nothing. Really. It's not you. That call. I didn't expect to—" He stopped. "Look, we said what we needed to say last night, didn't we?

Is there really anything else to discuss? We made mistakes, both of us. I don't think we need to relive them any further."

Her voice wavered. "But you said that meeting here would be okay."

"I know, and that was wrong," he said. "I'm sorry. I've had a lot going on in my life lately and I really did think it would be good to talk about whatever else it was you wanted to talk about. Get some closure on all of this." He looked back to the payphone. "I think I've had maybe enough closure for today."

"You can't go," she said.

"Izzy, don't make me be the bad guy here. Again. I don't want to, need to, or have to explain to you why I'm leaving. I am. Be okay with that, please."

"I deserve that. I do. I have no right to ask you to tell me anything about yourself, what that call was about, why you're here now after so many years. Any of it. But I have something I need to say to you. No. Something I *have* to say to you. Something I owe you to make right what I was too wrapped up in myself to realize that I'd done to you. To make right the hurt I caused."

Robert looked at his watch. "Look, I get it. Honestly though, I'd just rather we both get on with our lives. Let's consider each other forgiven and move on." He paused then put his hands on her shoulders and gave her cheek a light kiss. "Be good."

"Please don't," she whispered as he pulled away. Robert heard the pain in her voice and he resisted the urge to hug her goodbye. He didn't want to be cruel but she wasn't giving him a choice. The last thing he wanted was to give her hope.

"Bye," he said, as he walked around and past her. As he did, he came upon a young man sitting at a bench who looked familiar, though he hadn't the slightest idea as to why. Isabel call out behind him with an earnest despair.

"Bobby!"

Her tone stopped Robert. He turned, and as he did, the young man on the bench stood up next to him.

"What?" they both shouted back.

They looked at each other, then back to Isabel as she ran towards them.

CHAPTER
FOURTEEN

Bobby pretended not to watch Isabel when she looked over her shoulder to see if he was. Once she had turned away, he didn't take his eyes off of her. She approached an older black man at the outside of the rink. They embraced, though awkwardly, then made their way back to Bobby, but not arm-in-arm, not holding hands.

Who was this guy to her? What did it have to do with him?

Bobby squinted as they approached. The man's face passed in and out of shadows cast by the archway formed by the bare branches arcing over the path. He had never seen him before, yet his face had a familiarity he couldn't place. They were yards away when he stepped away from Isabel to make a call. He watched his mother rock back and forth on her heels. She looked over her shoulder again and Bobby swiveled his head quickly in the other direction. He wondered why he cared whether or not she saw him watching, but something about the moment felt voyeuristic, as if he saw her in a light that she didn't want to be seen. So he looked away and stole glances towards her until he saw it was safe.

When the man returned to her, something about their dynamic had changed. They spoke only briefly and he left her where she stood. Whatever she had planned, it had not gone well. Crestfallen, her arms hung limp by her sides. Bobby stared at the man as he approached and their eyes met. As they did, Bobby saw a recognition in the man's eyes, similar to what he felt when he'd seen his face.

Then he heard his mother yell his name.

He stood.

The man stopped.

They both answered her call.

Isabel jogged the short distance to meet them. Bobby and the man exchanged confused glances then both looked to Isabel. Bobby saw fear in her face.

"Mom, what's wrong?"

"Mom?" Robert asked her. "You have a son?"

"Yes," she said.

"Mom, what the hell is going on? Who is this guy?"

Tears streamed down her face. "I thought I could say it, but I can't."

"Izzy, what's happening here? What can't you say?"

"Oh, God," she said. "God, Robert, he's your son. You're his father. Oh, God, I'm so sorry."

Bobby knit his brow, then opened his eyes wide. The familiarity he'd seen in the man's face wasn't because he *knew* him, except he did, and that wasn't possible. He took a step back, the backs of his legs hitting the bench, and he sat. He stared at his feet and squished the pile of dirty slush beneath them. The first time Bobby had ever been punched, his head felt as if it were underwater, a pressure in his ears that muffled the sounds around him and made the swishing of blood as loud as rough rapids. He felt that same pressure now.

He's *dead*. That's what she'd told him, dead before he was born.

Dead, dead, dead.

Was that boy dead? God, they'd left him there bleeding and moaning. He'd left him there. He drove away.

The pressure swelled in his ears and moved behind his eyes and the edges seemed to dim. His cheeks felt numb. He put his face in his hands and shut his eyes. And he listened.

"What did you say?" Robert asked.

"We have a son."

"We have a son," he said.

"We have a son," Isabel repeated. Robert shouted an irritated laugh. He stepped closer to Isabel and talked quietly.

"Don't let me ever see either of you again," he said. "Do you understand me?" There was a threatening tone to his voice and the pressure in Bobby's ears faded. His cheeks tingled, warmed with the rush of blood. He watched them both closely, though his mind worked to process the surreal scene unfolding in front of him.

"I understand you're upset," Isabel said. "I know this is crazy."

"Was it the name tag?" he asked. His volume raised. People watched the three of them as they walked past, attempting surreptitiousness, but failing. "Was that it? I knew I should have taken it off when I came in to the bar."

"I don't know what you mean," Isabel said.

"You saw 'M.D.' on my badge and smelled money, didn't you?"

"What? No. Wait, what are you trying to say?"

"Don't bullshit me." People stopped pretending not to look and listen. "I'm sorry, I really am, that you couldn't keep track of whoever your kid's father is. Truly. And I'm sorry that people like you seem to just pop kids out whenever you'd like without even trying when people like me, who are educated and have the means to take care of them and raise them in a good home with loving parents have babies who die when their heartbeat just started."

Isabel's face collapsed. "You lost your baby?" She took a step toward him and he jerked away.

"Don't," he said. He wiped at his eye with his thumb. Isabel stepped back with her hands in the air. He pointed at Bobby but he wouldn't look at him. "That boy could be anyone's and you know it. How can you leverage your child for money from me? What kind of person does that? What I told you meant nothing last night? You decided you'd hurt me one more time."

"You're supposed to be dead," Bobby whispered to his feet.

"What?" Robert snapped, turning to face Bobby.

"She told me about you, she did. But she said you were dead. That you left before I was born, and that you died."

Robert turned to Isabel, eyes wide and incredulous.

"I was so angry," Isabel said, her voice quavering, "I wanted him to be angry with you, too. Except he wasn't. The older he got, the more he wanted to know about you. He had no reason to think you were…that he was…when he was born looking how he looked, with us living with my dad, I…" Her face reddened and she dropped her gaze. "It was just easier to keep up the lie. He kept pushing and asking so I had to tell him you were dead. I couldn't risk him asking the wrong questions in front of my father. God, I was so relieved that he looked white that I had to let him keep thinking it. I thought it would make things less complicated. Except it didn't. Not by a long shot. By the time he found about you, about your being…"

"Black, Isabel," Robert said. "Jesus Christ, quit dancing around it like it's profanity."

"I'm sorry," she said. "You're right. By the time he found that out, he had already started to believe things that he shouldn't, things I couldn't make right because it was already too late."

"What kind of things? Why couldn't you make it right?"

Isabel looked down again. "You know what, and you know why. Because he's got too much of his grandfather in him."

Robert took a step back, then dropped in the seat on the bench next to Bobby. "How could you do this? How could you lie to him? To me?"

Bobby looked up. "Lie to you?" he asked Robert. Bobby stared at Robert then at Isabel. She looked up to the sky and covered her mouth, turning away from them both. Bobby looked back to Robert. "Wait, you really didn't leave when she got pregnant?"

Robert glared at Isabel. "Leave? I never knew you existed until this moment. Right now."

Bobby put his face in his hands, resting his elbows on his knees. He shook his head back and forth.

"Bobby," Isabel said.

Bobby screamed into his hands. "Fuck."

Isabel and Robert jumped, as did a family that happened by at the time and the father hurried them along. Robert stood and so did Bobby. He needed to see for himself. His eyes traced Robert's face, the contour of his nose, the shape of his chin, the russet brown of his eyes, and he understood the familiarity that struck him the moment he saw him, the color of their skin their only real difference. Robert stood before him another version of himself, and he could see the same confused realization in Robert's eyes. The pressure drained from Bobby's ears and eyes, the blood returned to his limbs, heavy to counter the weightlessness and held him to the earth. He'd heard the desperate honesty in Robert's voice, an anger laced with sadness and more than a little regret. He truly hadn't known. Yet here he was, at a time when Bobby needed a father, *his* father, more than ever.

But him?

Bobby dropped down to the bench, his head back in his hands.

"Baby…" Isabel said.

Bobby looked up, his eyes tight with rage. "You need to not fucking talk to me right now."

Isabel took a step back, her eyes wet in an instant. Robert looked back and forth between them.

"Hey, wait a minute, man," Robert said to Bobby.

"No," Isabel said. "He's right. I should…I'm going to go."

"Good," Bobby said, with a petulance he had neither the desire nor the ability to control. Robert turned his back to Bobby, but around him, Bobby saw Isabel mouth the word "talk" to him as she made her way down the path and out of the park. Robert held his hands out to the side in a plea for her to stay, but they dropped to his sides as she turned into a dot in the distance. He sat back down next to Bobby.

"You think that might have been a little rough?" Robert asked him.

"Yeah, like you didn't want to say the exact same thing."

Robert laughed. "Fair enough."

"This is pretty fucked up."

"I'd say this is the definition of that, yeah."

They both laughed in grudging agreement, then sat forward, rubbing their hands. Bobby noted the similarity in their tic and sat back against the bench.

"So when did you know?"

Bobby tilted his head quizzically.

"That you were black."

"I'm not black."

"There's a few billion people who would beg to disagree with you."

"Yeah, well the only way they would know would be to ask. And

I'm sure as shit not telling." Bobby stood and walked away.

Robert followed.

"I'm asking. So tell me. Tell me about when you found out."

CHAPTER FIFTEEN

Bobby was eleven. He and Isabel had been living at his Grandpap's since he was born. He'd been lonely since his grandmother, Nina, died. Grandpap had to wait for Bobby at the bus stop and put him to bed when Isabel wasn't home. She worked a lot back then, trying to save up enough to put them into a decent apartment, somewhere that put Bobby in a good public school. But sometimes she stayed out too long. Just one drink after work, something to take the edge off. Grandpap told her if she wanted to stay, she had to hold down a job, pay into the mortgage, and quit her drinking. He didn't spend his years on the force cleaning up switchblade fights between the Micks and Spicks to waste his pension on his drunk of a daughter and her bastard kid. Still, though he pretended to be burdened by them both, even at that age, Bobby could tell Grandpap liked having them around.

Summer days they'd sit on rusted white steel chairs on Grandpap's porch covered in fake plastic grass. His tray-table ashtray overflowed with butts. He talked about the state of the world and clinked his can of Iron City to Bobby's pop can. They chugged and belched together. Grandpap made Bobby take a sip of his beer. Bobby held back a gag and hoped he didn't notice. Bobby pretended to like it and pulled it away from Grandpap when he asked for it back, an approving smile deepening the creases in his face, making Bobby feel safe—even loved. Though he didn't quite understand the feeling, he knew he wanted more of it, so he faked his understanding of what Grandpap talked about and he always, *always* agreed with everything he said, because he'd muss up Bobby's hair and call him a good boy when he did. He told him he was turning into a man because he understood man things.

Bobby understood why it was funny to wonder out loud if Sally Ride slowed down the trip into space by stopping to ask for directions.

He understood that Reagan had to do something, and fast, about the towel-heads bombing the U.S. Embassy in Beirut.

And he understood how nothing spoke to the decline of our country like a nigger Miss America.

The more Grandpap talked, the smarter he seemed to Bobby. There was nothing he didn't know, and it made Bobby feel lucky to have learned well enough to shut up and listen, because if he was lucky, he knew he'd turn out to be half the man Grandpap was.

He knew that because Grandpap said so.

One especially hot afternoon, they stayed inside all day. Bored with Spider-Man reruns, Bobby snuck outside while Grandpap slept in his recliner, another Iron City hanging precariously from his fingertips. The humidity filled Bobby's lungs and he patted his empty short pockets. He'd left his inhaler inside, but he didn't want to go back in and risk waking Grandpap. He had told him not go outside alone, especially in the alley.

Don't want to get caught alone with those hoodlums down the street, he'd said.

Bobby would nod dutifully, though this was one of the lessons Bobby struggled to understand.

The "hoodlums" were the grandchildren of an elderly black couple a few houses down the block that stayed with them during the summer months. They wore shirts and ties to church and helped their grandmother with her groceries. They tossed around a football and always apologized when it ended up in Grandpap's patch of lawn. They sat on their porch steps and read comics. And just then, they were in the back alleyway, and they looked like they were having fun.

They laughed hysterically and slapped each other five. Fourteen-year-old Darius, the eldest of the brothers, held the hips of an invisible someone and humped the air. He wore a mesh tank top and his forehead was covered in a sheen of sweat. Miles and Kevin, his two younger brothers, right around Bobby's age, giggled at his charades until they couldn't breathe. Kevin looked up and wiped tears from his eyes, and when he saw Bobby, he waved him over while they all signaled for Bobby to be quiet, in possession of some secret to tell.

Bobby looked back towards Grandpap's house. He remembered the beer can slipping out of his hand, like a long fuse on a stick of cartoon dynamite. He hadn't come storming out the door yet. It had to have fallen by now, and he still hadn't come looking for him. He knew he shouldn't join these boys, but something stronger than Grandpap's admonitions pulled at him. The boys looked so excited to see him. He had no other friends in the neighborhood and he wanted to have fun, too.

When he reached them, he saw they had an issue of Penthouse. Bobby recognized Vanessa Williams from the television press conference when they took away her Miss America crown. Miles and Kevin grabbed Bobby by his arms, shook them with their excitement until they felt limp, and asked him if he'd ever seen a naked woman before. Bobby felt a throbbing in his shorts, and he thought by the way they asked him that they most certainly had, so he gave a nonchalant nod and crinkled his chin like it was no big deal. Miles and Kevin held out their hands for a high-five. Bobby hesitated, then happily obliged.

Grandpap's block was filled with people just like him, grumpy and medicinal-smelling when they crowded Bobby in the pews at church. There were never any kids, at least none that he'd been allowed to play with. He'd made Bobby terrified of these boys, but in that moment, he felt he'd known them his entire life.

Maybe Grandpap didn't know *everything*.

"Where did you get this?" Bobby asked. "I mean, are we supposed to be looking at this?" The three brothers stopped laughing and looked at each other, then back to Bobby.

"Hell, yeah!" they said in unison. Darius explained that when he took the trash out, the bag snagged and ripped and the magazine fell out of the bottom. They guessed it was their grandfather's and Darius made a jerking motion in the air. Miles and Kevin made gagging noises and burst into laughter again, then shushed each other for being too loud. Bobby laughed, too, then looked back again to Grandpap's house.

They flipped through the photos, beginning to end and then back again. Miles and Kevin boasted about how she should be their woman, and Darius checked them, telling them they wouldn't know what to do with her. They shot back that he didn't even have a girlfriend, how would he know. Bobby even joined in, and Miles and Kevin howled. Darius did, too. Then his tone became more serious.

"Not right what they did to her, though," said Darius. His brothers shook their heads and sucked at their teeth in disappointed agreement.

"What do you mean?" Bobby asked.

"Not letting her be Miss America. That's not right. Nana said she needs to get some church in her, but they would have never done that to her if she was white."

Bobby was confused. Maybe they didn't understand how things were. How Grandpap told him they were supposed to be.

"But she's supposed to be white," Bobby said. "A nigger can't be Miss America."

Darius's arms dropped to his sides. The wrinkled magazine hung from his fingers by a partially torn page. Bobby became aware of the intense heat, the smell of cut grass, the high whine of a weed-whacker a few houses down. Sweat trickled into his ear but under Darius's stare, he dared not move.

Why? What had he said wrong? Why did Darius seem so angry?

Bobby glanced to Kevin and Miles. They didn't look as angry as Darius. Their eyes went from Bobby to Darius and back again, frightened. Bobby was scared, too. Why hadn't he listened to Grandpap? His words echoed.

Stand your ground.

They'll stab you in the back.

Never run away, never look away.

Bobby looked back to Darius and returned his glare. The page tore through and the magazine dropped to the ground. Bobby never saw him swing.

Light flashed behind his eyes. They filled with water and the blood in his mouth tasted hot and metallic. His nose throbbed. He'd never been hit before, but he told himself not to cry. Miles and Kevin looked on in shock. They whispered to their brother to be calm, to come inside with them. Darius stood in front of Bobby, shoulders heaving, hands balled up, waiting for Bobby to move. To say something else.

Bobby turned on his heel and yelled for Grandpap. He saw the screen door open and Grandpap look down the alleyway, at Bobby running towards him. He ducked back in and then reappeared quickly, limping down the back steps to meet his grandson. Bobby saw the sun catch something in his hand. He wiped the tears from his eyes and skidded to a stop in the gravel when he saw Grandpap's old service revolver.

The brothers saw it too and yelled. They ran back into their house. Grandpap put his arm around Bobby and led him inside.

Isabel was in the kitchen when they returned. When she saw Bobby, she screamed. Grandpap sat him in a chair and told Bobby to pinch his nose and tilt his head back. Blood ran down the back of this throat. Isabel squatted in front of him and touched at the bridge of his nose. She winced when he hissed in pain but pressed at it again like she didn't believe it was real and had to touch it again to be sure. Grandpap handed Bobby a dishrag filled with ice.

"Quit your shrieking and leave him be," he said. "Boy's fine."

"This is what happens when I leave him home alone with you?" she said. She pressed the ice firmly to his nose and he whimpered. "Oh, baby, I'm sorry."

"What are you even doing here?" Grandpap asked. "I said leave him be. He can hold his own ice. He's all right."

"Work was slow and they asked who wanted to go home," she said. "I figured I'd come home and spend time with my baby. What the hell happened? You're supposed to be watching him. And don't you dare tell me what to do with my son."

"Don't yell at me, girl. And don't pretend you came right home, either."

"What?" Isabel asked.

"I can smell it on you," Grandpap said. "That's what."

He was right. Even with his blood-clogged nose, Bobby smelled that familiar sweet-sour odor. He pulled his face away from her touch. She tilted her head and reached for him again but he pulled back further, much to her confusion. Bobby held the ice to his nose and tilted his head back. It throbbed every time his heart beat.

"So I stopped for a drink on the way," she said to Grandpap. "One."

"It's the middle of the day," Grandpap said.

"And how many have you had so far, Dad? Huh? Were you passed out? Again? Where was he? Who did this to him?"

Bobby's head pulsed. From the punch. From the shouting. He was angry that he still felt so scared, and scared about how angry he was, with himself for not listening to stay away from those boys, with Isabel for yelling at the man who protected him, kept him safe better than she ever had. Late or not, he was *there*. She was at the bar. The thought enraged him and he spit the answer to her question.

"It was those niggers down the street!"

Isabel slapped him hard, then jerked back the same hand and covered her mouth. She reached both hands out for his face and apologized. Bobby cried so hard his ribs hurt. It wasn't just the punch to the face. It was all the nights he'd put himself to bed and the mornings she wasn't there. Bobby shook with ragged sobs. She couldn't calm him down. The only word he could utter was "why?"

Why did you hit me? Why are you never home? Why did you have to drink so much? Over and over, "why" poured forth like a fire hydrant opened up in the middle of the street. Grandpap grabbed Isabel and pulled her to her feet.

"What the hell did you hit him for?" he shouted.

"This is what you teach him?" she asked. "No wonder he got punched!"

"Save your hippy bullshit, Isabel." He lifted Bobby's head by his chin. "Calm down, calm down," he said to Bobby. Bobby snuffled and wiped at his nose but he couldn't stop crying. "Come on, you're all right. Took your lumps like a man, I'll tell you that much. Don't you listen to your mother. You didn't do anything wrong."

"Yes, he did," Isabel shouted. "You can't make him think it's okay to talk like that, to think like that. Like you."

He turned from Bobby and walked Isabel down putting her back up against the stove. "I put a roof over your head, food in this kid's mouth, and try to teach him to be a man, and Lord knows this boy needs it. What do you do? You aren't even here half the time, and when you could be, you're getting drunk."

She glanced at Bobby, then back to Grandpap with a look that said not to say those things in front of him. He looked back at Bobby, then back to her and laughed.

"What, you think he doesn't know why you're never here? That it's all just work? Go ahead, ask him. Ask him what he thinks about you. Don't you want to know?"

Isabel looked down at her feet. Grandpap bent his knees to make eye contact but she kept moving her head away from him.

"Yeah, that's what I thought," he said. He lifted her chin to make her look at him. "He needs a man in his life. To tell him the way things are. So you tell me why it's so bad if this kid turns out even a little bit like me. Hell, he's the boy I should have had."

At that, Isabel's face changed. The shame went away.

"You want to know why it's terrible if he turns out like you?" Isabel asked. Her lips pulled back from her teeth, a cornered wolf. "Because his father was a nigger."

Bobby pulled the ice away from his face and his crying stopped. Grandpap took a step back and let out a laugh that sounded more like a shout.

"Bullshit," he said. "That boy's as white as I am."

Isabel stepped towards him and wiped tears from her eyes. "Look at me," she said, pointing at her face. "Tell me I'm lying."

Grandpap's smile faded. She looked past him to where Bobby sat shell-shocked. She mouthed "I'm sorry."

Bobby's ears rang and his jaw ached.

Grandpap backhanded Isabel. It cracked so loud that Bobby thought he broke either his hand or her face. She fell back against the stove and put her hand to her cheek. Bobby launched himself at him and pounded on his wide back. Grandpap reached back with his thick hand and palmed Bobby's face. Isabel screamed for him not to touch him and pushed him aside. She wrapped her arms around Bobby and pulled him down to the floor with her. Bobby spun around and slapped at her. He caught her in the same reddened patch of skin where Grandpap hit her. She dropped to her rear end and held her face again. Bobby stood over her with his hands balled up. His shoulders heaved and his chest tightened.

A metallic clatter came from the front of the house and all heads turned. A police officer stood on the porch and pounded on the screen door. Darius's grandmother stood behind him. Grandpap cursed to himself. He stored his pistol in its case and returned it to the top shelf of his pantry. He jabbed a finger in the air towards Isabel.

"I'll deal with you in a minute," he said under his breath. He smoothed back his thin white strands, then called out to the officer at the screen door by his first name. Bobby ran from the kitchen and up the stairs. On his way out, Isabel whispered, "Robert."

CHAPTER SIXTEEN

"Grandpap knew the cop who came to the door. Basically made it out like the kid's grandma was hysterical, making the whole thing up. He even flipped it around, said he should have called the cops on her grandson for assault."

"Did he?" Robert asked.

"Nah," Bobby said. He half-smiled at Robert. "He had other things on his mind."

"Yeah, I guess so."

Bobby lit a cigarette and offered his pack to Robert. He waved it off, but then grabbed for the pack before Bobby could take it away. Bobby struck a match and shielded the flame from the breeze. They inhaled and exhaled simultaneously. "So then what?"

"We left," Bobby said. "Mom wasn't having it anymore. Stuffed my clothes and comics into a gym bag and left." Bobby laughed to himself.

165

"What?"

"He didn't even try to stop us. He practically raised me. And you know what he said on our way out the door?" Robert shook his head. "Nothing. Not one word."

"Did that make you angry?"

"You know what made me mad? So we're driving away, and I can't even look at Mom, let alone talk to her. So I dig in my bag to find my favorite comic. This X-Men annual with some cheesy villain in it named Horde. But it's kind of a spotlight on Wolverine, so I'm in, you know?"

Robert shrugged. "Who doesn't love Logan?"

Bobby leaned away from Robert in surprise. "You were into comics?"

"Were?" he said. "Am."

"Huh," Bobby said. "Anyway, I'm paging through it and I stop on this panel I never gave much thought to before. Wolverine kisses Storm. I tossed it in the backseat and never read it again. That's the shit that made me mad. Not Grandpap letting us leave. That Mom had done what she had done and lied to him."

"Seeing Ororo and Logan kiss," Robert said. "It made you think about your mother and me. Made you think about the thing that made you lose your grandfather. Is that why you decided to pass for white all this time?"

"Wouldn't you?"

"Bobby," he said, then stopped. He shook his head and laughed to himself.

"Weird, right?" Bobby said.

Robert nodded. "I'm a physician. Busted my ass to get to where I am. But there isn't a day that goes by that I don't look in the mirror that I don't see a black man before I see a doctor. Because I have to. To survive. I'm a damn doctor, Bobby, but that's what I have to do to survive. In order to keep myself safe, I have to remember that there's a lot of your Grandpaps out there, who see me the same way. Black *first*. Not remembering that can get me killed. And I think you know that. You know why?"

Bobby shook his head.

"Because I think every day, you do the same thing. I think you look in that mirror and tell yourself you're white because you think it's what *you* have to do to survive. That it's what makes you happy and keeps you safe."

Bobby looked away from Robert.

"Can I ask you something?" Robert said.

Bobby kept his face averted from Robert but nodded.

"Has it made you happy?"

Bobby shook his head.

"Has it kept you safe?"

A tear fell from Bobby's eye. Then another. He shook his head and wiped at his face with his sleeve. He heard a beeping sound and turned to see Robert leaning back to unclip a pager from his waist. Robert read the screen and dropped his head with a sigh. "Oh, come on," he whispered.

"What?"

"Kid they brought in two nights ago. Somebody caved his head in with a brick. We'd gotten him stabilized, but he wasn't out of the woods. He just died. God damn it, I just saw him last night."

Bobby felt the top of his head go hot. He willed the sweat away from his forehead and denied the bile roiling in his stomach from rocketing into his mouth, where his tongue now felt covered in paste, clinging to the roof of his mouth.

"Do they know who did it?" Bobby said.

Robert shook his head. "Not that I've heard, but they're looking. Probably going to be looking a bit harder now." Robert's eyes narrowed. "You all right?"

"Me? Why?"

"I don't know," Robert said, "you seem a bit, I don't know. Provoked."

"Can you blame me?" Bobby laughed, a bit too loudly. He noticed Robert notice.

"I don't suppose I can," Robert said. "I should get to the hospital. His family is likely on their way there." They both stood. The feeling of lightness returned, and Bobby pushed the backs of his knees against the bench to steady himself. "Do you need a ride, or..."

"No," Bobby said. "I'm going to catch the bus." They fidgeted, hands going from pockets, to arms crossed, shifting weight from foot to foot. "Listen, there's something I have to do now. Something I have to take care of and I'm honestly not sure how it's going to turn out. I know that sounds mysterious and what not. But this." He pointed back and forth between the two of them. "Can we do this again? Talk?"

"Yeah," Robert said, turning up the corner of his mouth. "Yeah, we can do that."

Bobby scrawled his address on the matchbook and handed it to Robert. "Tomorrow, late morning sometime?"

Robert nodded, took the matchbook. Bobby stuck out his hand for a shake. Robert looked at it, then moved it to the side as he stepped towards him. He put his arms under Bobby's and wrapped them around his back in a tight embrace. Bobby's arms hung in the air but Robert held on. Bobby drew Robert closer, and Robert placed his hand on the back of Bobby's head, pulling his face to his chest. Bobby paused there, tense, then let go and wept. He shook with sobs, his breath almost ragged. Robert shushed him and pulled him closer still.

"Breathe," Robert told him.

A toxic reservoir of fear and anger, resentment and sorrow, emptied from Bobby with each tearful exhale, but each inhale brought something new: safety. He felt safe. Though Bobby was a grown man, Robert's arms felt strong and secure. Protective, the way he always thought a father's should, the way he'd always wished his mother's would. Though he was terrified of what he knew he had to do now to make things right, his father was here.

Bobby calmed and he and Robert stood back from each other. Robert wiped a tear from his own eye. They gave each other a tight-lipped nod and walked away. Bobby turned.

"Hey, I'm sorry," he said. "That you lost your baby. Did you know if it was a boy or a girl?"

Robert shook his head no. "Thank you. When you see your mother tonight, go easy, huh? Talk to her."

Bobby nodded and gave a half-hearted wave as he walked in the direction of the bus stop.

"You're either really early or really late," the bistro hostess said to Bobby as she held the door open. He'd missed the chance to pick up a lunch shift, but it was too early for the second shift to filter in, so he headed up to the smoking section. His stomach growled. In all that had happened in the last few hours, he'd been too lost in his head to realize he hadn't eaten. He decided to make use of the employee discount while he waited to send someone home for the night. He wondered if Aaron would be working.

When he reached the top of the steps, he saw Michelle. She sipped a soda and read a textbook. When she saw Bobby, she rolled her eyes and went back to her book. He sat at the two-top next to her, their backs to each other. Bobby fished for his cigarettes but had given the matchbook to Robert.

"Hey," he said. Without looking up from her book Michelle

reached back and handed him a jet-black zippo with a Misfits skull logo. He lit up and her arm shot backwards again, opening and closing her hand impatiently until he dropped the lighter back into her palm.

"Thanks," he said. She grunted. A Flock of Seagulls drifted from the overhead speakers. He laughed to himself as "I'd Run So Far Away" played. Not a terrible idea, he thought.

"The Eighties station," he said to Michelle's back. "Russell must be the manager on duty again. He's the only one who likes this crap." She flipped to the next page in her book and gave an exasperated sigh. They sat in silence until the server brought Michelle her food and took Bobby's order.

"Can I ask you something?" he said.

"I'm studying," she said.

"Okay, cool. Sorry."

Flock of Seagulls faded into "Take On Me."

"I'm asking Russell to put me with another trainer tonight," she said.

Another server brought Bobby chicken fingers and fries. Ravenous, he stuffed his face. "I'm not even on tonight," he mumbled through a mouthful of food. "Just trying to pick up a shift. But it's cool, I get it."

"Do you?" she asked.

"What do you mean?"

"I mean that bullshit last night with you and your boy, Aaron. Is that really what you're all about?"

Bobby stopped chewing and looked out into the restaurant as if the right answer to her question rested somewhere in the plastic decorations and retro movie posters that hung all over the restaurant. The right answer couldn't be found, however. There simply wasn't one.

"After the last few hours, I couldn't begin to tell you what I'm all about," Bobby said. "Truth be told, I don't know if I could before, either."

Michelle stood up with her plate of food in hand and sat in the chair next to Bobby. Her straight black hair fell over her right eye. She tucked it behind her ear but it slid forward and back into her face so that she had to repeatedly pull it back. Bobby wanted to ask her why she cut her hair that way if it meant always having to do that, but he wanted her to stay. Tonight, she had a blue gemstone in her nostril and one of those hoops through her nose like a bull. Bobby ran his tongue over his teeth to make sure there was nothing in them. She tucked her hair behind her ear again.

"How do you not know?" she said. "You either are or you aren't."

"Aren't what?" Bobby asked. "I'm confused."

"Yeah," she said. "I think you are."

"Can we start this over? I have no idea what you're talking about now."

She leaned forward. "I was right, wasn't I?" she asked. "You're mixed, huh?"

Bobby sat straight up and looked over his shoulders to see who might have heard. Despite the reunion with Robert, Bobby didn't want anyone else to know. Not yet. He'd made no secret of his feelings about waiting on black tables because of what they ordered, how they behaved, or how little they tipped. He'd be subject to no small amount of humiliation if he didn't reveal his truth on his own terms, if at all.

The server working their section leaned against the bus stand and rubbed at his nose with his knuckle, trying to pick it without looking like he was trying to pick it. Too far away to hear.

He looked past Michelle and down the steps to the main dining room, not far from where they sat. No one there, either. She craned her neck to get in his face, not confrontational, but not letting

171

him look away, no spite in her eyes, just an intense curiosity, even something that looked like understanding.

In just two days, Bobby's life had flipped like a film negative. That which should have been light, now darkened. Perspectives changed. Colors reversed. It had been so easy to pass before Bobby met Aaron because then he only had to lie to himself. He was Beast in the first issue of X-Men, still a mutant, but hiding in plain sight, never to be discovered unless he took off his shoes and revealed his mutant feet. When Aaron and Bobby met, with Aaron trying so hard to be his version of black, Bobby could feel the hairy blue mutation of Beast trying to break through, so he had to be careful not to slip. He never brought Aaron around Isabel. Bobby tried to shame him for pretending to be like "them", when "them" was "him."

He watched Michelle continue to look to him for an answer. The day left had him tired, but optimistic, protective, and yet somewhat vulnerable.

He nodded.

"I knew it!" She slapped the table. He gestured for her to lower her voice and saw that his hand shook, though it wasn't because he was afraid. He felt light, like he did in the park, like the head rush of that first cigarette when he hadn't eaten all day. Unburdened. Michelle leaned back in her chair with her arms crossed over her stomach, satisfied but still curious. "Why the act, then?" she asked.

"What do you mean?" Bobby asked.

"Black folks not tipping. All the crap Aaron said last night."

"That's not an act," Bobby said.

"Well, no, not for him, I know."

"Yeah, not for me, either."

She puffed air through her lips. "That's jacked up." The fire went out of Bobby's hot air balloon at the sound of the judgment in her voice and he stood up to leave. "Wait, what happened?" she asked.

"Where are you going?"

"This was a mistake. You know what? I was lying to fuck with you. Ha, ha, big joke, you fell for it. Forget I said anything."

She pulled on Bobby's wrist and motioned for him to sit. She still had that look, like she didn't mean any harm, so he sat back down.

"I've never told anyone that," he said. "Ever. So maybe there's more to it. Maybe dial back the judgment." He held up his thumb and index finger. "Just a little."

"You're right," she said. "I'm sorry."

Bobby took a puff from his inhaler. His lungs relaxed but the medicine gave him jitters on top of what he already felt so he fished out another cigarette and sparked up. Michelle rested her cheek in her hand.

"What?" he asked.

"Tell me," she said.

"Tell you what?"

"You said there's more to it. Tell me everything."

He did. He couldn't help himself. He told her about Isabel's drinking. Living with Grandpap. The fight in the alley and the first time he found about his father. The night they got kicked out. How he learned at too young an age to position Isabel at night when her snores didn't sound right so she wouldn't choke on her own puke. He told her about how he met Aaron and how he lost him to prison. How between working almost every day since before he was even old enough to do so and Mom's diner tips that they were sometimes able to make the rent on time. And he told her after twenty-two years, just hours ago, he'd met the father he'd thought abandoned them, the father he thought was dead.

Michelle never spoke. She hung on every word.

Bobby slumped back in his chair. He felt like the first time he finished the mile in gym class, exhausted but exhilarated. When he looked at his watch, he was shocked to see he'd been talking for more than an hour. Michelle dragged her fingers under her eyes and grabbed a napkin to blot away her mascara. She heard him, listened to him, and she didn't judge him. He'd removed the sack of bricks from his shoulder and poured them all out on the table for her, but there was still one stuck on the bottom, all twisted up in the fabric that wouldn't come out. Until he did that, he'd never feel free, though shaking that brick loose would likely remove any chance at real freedom. When he finished, they both let out a deep breath at the same time and laughed. They went to speak at the same time and laughed again.

"You go ahead," she said.

Do it. You've told her everything else. Tell her everything. She asked.

"I think I've said enough," he said.

"Go on."

"I've just never said any of that shit out loud," Bobby said. "And now I've done it twice. It's like I stepped back and was watching someone who looked like me say it."

"So why tell me?" she said. "Your dad, I get. Why trust me?"

"Because you asked?"

"I'm being serious."

"Me, too." He truly didn't know. After last night, she'd had every reason to run around the smoking section, laughing and pointing at Bobby, outing him. But when she didn't, the rest of the story just came. It took her asking for him to figure why he told her everything and it was a harsh realization.

"I guess I told you because I don't have anyone else." She scrunched her mouth and Bobby saw pity. "Don't do that."

"Do what?" she asked.

"Look at me like I'm some stray puppy." His voice grew louder. "I'm fine."

"I never said you weren't," she said. Her tone stayed even and low. Bobby shook his soft pack for another cigarette but only tobacco shavings fell into his hand. Michelle pulled two from her pack and lit them both in her mouth and handed him one.

"So let me ask you something," he said.

"Go ahead."

"How did you decide? You know, how to be?"

"I don't follow," she said.

"You don't look white. But you talk pretty good."

"Well," she said. "I speak well."

He rolled his eyes. "Whatever. You know what I mean."

"I don't think I do," she said.

"How did you decide what to be?" he asked. "Come on, don't make this weird. Fine, how did you decide whether you wanted to be black or white?"

She sat back and laughed. "Oh, man. You're not just mixed. You're mixed up."

"Tell me something I don't know."

"Okay. I'm not mixed."

Bobby leaned forward in his seat and whispered. "Shut up. You're white?"

"What? No."

"Then what?"

"Black, dummy. Both my parents are black."

Bobby flopped back into his chair. "No way."

"Why is it so hard to believe?" she asked. "Because I'm 'light-skinned?'" She made air quotes. "Or is it because I 'speak so well'?"

"Both, really," Bobby said. "The way you talk, for sure."

She shook her head and stubbed out her cigarette. "So, until that day in the alley, you thought you were white, right?" Bobby nodded. "When you found out about your dad, did the way you talked change?

Did you come downstairs, grab your dick and be all 'Hey yo, Pops, me and Ma Dukes, we Audi. Five Thousand, G?'"

Bobby held back a laugh and shook his head. "That sounds even weirder when you say it."

"You know what I mean. You didn't start wearing your baseball hat sideways, and shell-top Adidas and listen to rap and—,"

"Okay, okay," he said. "I know what you're trying to say, but it was different for me. I'm different."

"You're not, though," she said. "You were black for years and didn't know it, but you didn't talk 'black.'" She made quotes in the air with her fingers. "You didn't dress 'black,' didn't do any of the things you think are black, because people, people like your grandfather told you that that's the way it's supposed to be. That if you're black, you automatically talk, dress and act a certain way. But you didn't then and you don't now. All of this, Bobby, this 'talking white' or 'acting black' nonsense? Some kind of racial programming to act a certain way? It's crap. Bullshit. And I think you know it. I think you always did."

She sat back and rubbed her hands on the top of her legs and looked at Bobby again as though she waited for him to talk. But he had nothing. Within minutes, she had eviscerated every excuse behind every piece of rhetoric he'd been fed until he convinced himself he believed it, her words adamantium claws to the guts of an enemy, spilling out onto the floor, desperately grabbing at their viscera to keep it within, while realizing the futility of it all. They both let out another deep breath and she stood.

"I have to pee," she said. "To be continued." She put a hand on Bobby's shoulder and let it linger for a brief second as she walked past and he turned to watch her walk away.

He couldn't wait for her to get back. He picked at the callouses on his hands again and wondered if this feeling was what kept Isabel going back to the booze, the lightness that all this honesty afforded him. He'd hidden himself for so long, he didn't know what it felt like to truly share something—share himself—with someone without worrying about being judged or the consequences of truth. He wasn't afraid of Michelle or what she would do with all these things he'd told her. Maybe he should have been. But the way she looked at him made him want to tell her more and more. Everything. The idea overwhelmed him and his eyes burned.

"God, you're such a weepy little bitch today," he said to himself. He looked up to grab a napkin from the other side of the table when he saw Aaron at the bottom of the steps. Staring. Standing there who knew how long.

Watching.

Listening.

He couldn't hear us, Bobby told himself. Not with Michelle in front of him and over the music and down at the bottom of the steps.

No fucking way.

God damn it, when did he get here?

Still he stared. Bobby waved to him and Aaron walked into the kitchen as though he'd been snapped from a trance. Bobby had hoped he'd be in tonight. The plan, putting the rest of the money in Aaron's pickup and then talking him into turning himself in and maybe even absolving Bobby, it all seemed like a solid plan, at least better than no plan at all. That was until Aaron appeared like some Goddamned eavesdropping ghost. Then the bottom fell out.

Bobby felt a hand on his shoulder and jumped. Michelle squeaked.

"Jesus," she said. "I washed my hands. Relax." Bobby gave a nervous laugh and she looked at him quizzically as she sat back down. She started talking again, but all Bobby saw were comic book conversation bubbles over her head, filled with shorthand symbols and squiggly lines. A thought cloud hung over Bobby's head where

Aaron's face morphed into the Red Skull, pointing a Luger at Bobby's head.

CHAPTER
SEVENTEEN

Bobby chewed on his thumbnail as he leaned against the edge of the busser's station. Michelle finished taking a drink order and came up to the computer.

"He didn't hear anything," she said.

"How do you know?" He took another pump from his inhaler.

"I've been meaning to ask you, how can you have asthma and smoke?" she asked.

"It's a talent. How do you know he didn't hear anything?"

She sighed and sent the order back to the kitchen, then leaned on the bus stand next to Bobby as they looked out over their station. "I don't," she said. "But come on. Over the music? Downstairs? And who knows how long he was even standing there? I'm sure it's fine. Just relax. You've got happier things to think about, anyway. Right? I mean, your dad. That's so crazy."

"Right," he said. "No problem."

She hadn't seen him standing there, immobile, sizing Bobby up. After Aaron disappeared into the kitchen, Bobby had asked Michelle if she'd changed her mind about shadowing him, and she had. He told her before they started the shift that he'd watch the station while she ran food. She didn't ask why, but he knew she'd known he was scared by the way she smiled at him. He asked for updates every time she came back from the kitchen. Did he seem mad? What was he saying? Did he say anything to her? She told Bobby that Russell was pissed that he wasn't running food and that every time he told her that, Aaron looked at her funny.

"Funny? Funny how?" he asked.

"Just weird, you know?"

"Weird like 'huh, I wonder why Bobby's not running food' or 'that little motherfucker's hiding and I'm going to kill him when I see him' weird? Which one?"

"Jesus, Bobby, how the hell should I know? I don't know the guy. Go find out yourself."

Bobby shook his head and chewed on his other thumbnail. Michelle ran the station. He leaned and chewed, chewed and leaned.

She's right. Settle the hell down. There's no way he would have heard us. I would have seen him standing down there. I totally would have.

Except he didn't. He had no idea Aaron stood there and he vomited his life story to this girl he hardly knew.

Jesus, I almost told her what we did to that kid.

He would have heard that, too, and there was no question in Bobby's mind about what he would have done if he had. None.

Bobby just wanted—needed—to know if Aaron had heard the truth about his father. Knowing would have been better than all this wondering. Wouldn't it? Maybe he wouldn't even have been upset. He'd find out eventually and they would have to talk about it.

But if he knows, he didn't find out from you. All he knows is that you lied to him, that you trusted a stranger with your truth before your trusted him.

Bobby took another puff from his inhaler. He hadn't felt an attack coming but the habit made him feel better. However, it was his fifth puff in an hour and his hands shook and the jitters made him more anxious, which made him need the inhaler more. Michelle came back to the bus station.

"You got the station for a minute?" he asked.

"I've had it for the last hour," she said. "Look, not that I've got any love lost for the guy, but did you stop to think that maybe if he heard, it'd be okay? I mean he *is* your best friend."

Bobby looked at her incredulously. "Get out my head, will you? And was. He *was* my best friend."

"Are you going to tell me what happened with you two?"

"I need a cigarette," he said. "You sure you got this?"

"You know you're going to have to walk past him to get to the dock," she said.

"Nuh-uh." Their station sat next to the door to the patio and Bobby pointed to it.

"Go," she said. "But hurry up. If Russell comes looking for you, that's your ass. I'm not getting canned."

Bobby fired her a sarcastic two thumbs up as he pushed his back against the door. A few inches of snow piled up on the porch and it took a few shoves to get outside. The cold air sucked in like he'd opened an airlock and customers down the row shot him pissed off looks while Michelle shook her head and waved him away. Bobby hopped the low fence and walked to the back of the building.

He lit one of the cigarettes Michelle had given him and spit into the snow. They were less harsh than his and tasted like shit, but they didn't trigger his asthma so he sucked it up. He thought about Isabel again. How he understood more and more why she drank, though this time for a different reason than the addictive feeling that came with his revelations. His own thoughts were driving him crazy. He wanted to go home and sit on the couch next to her, crack open a bottle of vodka and wait for morning to see Robert, to tell her, *show me how you do this, because I can't take it.*

He pushed open the chain link door to the loading dock. Since he'd avoided going through the kitchen he hadn't grabbed his jacket, and he rubbed the goose bumps on his arms in between inhalations. The back door from the kitchen swung open hard and Bobby jumped. His eyes were slow to adjust to the light he only saw the outline of someone standing in the door and he instantly regretted coming back here alone. His heart thumped so hard it made his ears feel plugged.

The door closed and Bobby's eyes focused. One of the bussers dragged two tall waste cans full of empty beer bottles behind him. Bobby propped himself against the fence and breathed out hard while the busser placed a wedge in the door to keep it from closing, The heat curtain blasted and masked the chaotic clanks and shouts of the kitchen. The busser dumped the first can. Bottles shattered as they smacked off of each other. Bobby turned away and looked through the fencing at the cars parked in the rear. He put his fingers through the holes and realized that this would be a view he might have to get used to. On the inside looking out, like he'd always lived his life. Bottles smashed as the busser emptied the second can and he flinched again.

Jesus, get it together.

The busser stacked the bins and went back inside but just before the door latched shut, someone pushed it back open.

Aaron walked out onto the dock.

He looked at Bobby in surprise. The wedge holding open the door was at his feet and he slid it under the closed door and kicked it home. Bobby thought he should have run when his back was turned but he had nowhere to go and no one to run to. Even if he got away from Aaron here, it would only be temporary, just delay things for a little while longer and he was so tired from being scared that he didn't want to wait for the end anymore.

Aaron lit up and inhaled. Neither of them spoke. They were Logan and Creed, Wolverine and Sabretooth, brothers but enemies, circling, waiting for the other to show his claws and attack.

Bobby felt for the wine key in the pocket of his apron as he had the night before, but found only the half-empty pack of smokes Michelle had given him. She hadn't gotten her wine key yet and he had loaned her his. He rolled his eyes and pulled out another cigarette.

If I got to go, I'm going to go smoking. Too bad I don't have a blindfold.

Aaron leaned against the wall next to the door and watched Bobby watch him.

Bobby knew Aaron was waiting him out, letting his fear build such that he'd blabber out the truth in terror of him so he could feel justified about whatever it was he was going to do. Bobby heard the *snikt* in his head as he showed his claws first.

"I don't know what you heard," Bobby said. "Or you think you heard." Aaron raised an eyebrow and blew smoke through his nose like a cartoon bull. "I don't have anyone to talk to, man, and this thing that we did, that *you* did to that kid, it's fucking killing me, Aaron." He began to tell him the kid had died, but stopped himself. How he knew would only lead to more questions. Aaron eyed him with the pause, so he continued. "I can't sleep, I hardly eat, and I feel like I'm having a constant asthma attack. I didn't tell her what happened, man, I swear to you I didn't."

Aaron stayed attached to the wall, dragging and exhaling. He looked past Bobby more than he looked at him. Bobby closed his eyes and took a deep breath.

"But I told her a lot of things, and if you heard it all and you hate me, then you hate me, but I can't change it, no matter how much I want to."

Aaron flicked his cigarette into the snow, and leaned against the fence next to Bobby. Bobby's muscles went on high alert, full fight-or-flight, waiting for the slightest movement from Aaron. He didn't stand a chance against Aaron physically but he wasn't going to go down without a fight. He was tired of being batted around like a catnip mouse. But under the dock light, Bobby saw Aaron's face in detail, and he looked scared, too.

"You were wrong last night," Aaron said. His voice shook. "When I pulled the gun? When you said this isn't about you. It *is* about you. It's *always* been about you. Everything that has anything to do with me as long as you've known me has always been about *you*." He breathed out hard like he'd just finished a race and took out another cigarette. The lighter shook in his hands and when the flame lit his face, Bobby saw tears in his eyes. Aaron really was scared. "It was about you from the day we met on the schoolbus. I knew right away that you'd end up being the best friend I'd ever had and that I would know you for the rest of my life. I hated school. I hated that my parents made me go to that school, where people like you and me were the minority. Where no matter how hard I tried to fit in, I got my ass kicked. Then you showed up and you called me on my shit and you stood up for me, fought for me, because of me, and you didn't have to. You were my hero, man. Even with your shitty taste in comic books."

They shared a short laugh.

"Aaron," Bobby said.

He held his hand up to stop Bobby and wiped at his eyes. "As bad as it was for us, I hated for the school day to end. I'd wish the weekend away to get to see you on Monday. I even started reading fucking Marvel comics." He laughed again, hoarse.

"I just knew you knew. You had to have known. How could you not? We were the Comic Book Queers, right?"

Bobby nodded.

"Do you remember what you said to me afterwards?"

Bobby nodded again but his shame kept his eyes downward.

"Yeah," Aaron said. "Me, too."

Bobby remembered what happened after, too. Aaron became distant, but it felt normal, the way guys grow apart without any thing necessarily gone wrong between them. After a short time, Bobby had forgotten about it. When they made it to high school and Aaron started dealing, Bobby saw him less and less. He had new friends. Bobby still only had Aaron, but he worked so much that between taking care of Isabel and making rent, he didn't really have time for anything else. Bobby didn't think too much about it. So easy for him; impossible, it seemed for Aaron. For all his size, leaning there against the fence, he looked broken. Bobby wanted to reach out to him and pull him in for a hug, but even now, he feared what he thought that might mean to Aaron and he felt ashamed of himself for being afraid. He thought about telling him that he wasn't alone in his secrets. If he told him, he'd maybe feel that same conflict of wanting to pretend it didn't bother him.

But then again maybe he wouldn't.

Maybe he'd find the nearest blunt object and smash Bobby in the face.

"Aaron."

"You want to know why I did it, Bobby? Because when my cellmate came for me the first night in prison, he took something that didn't belong to him. Something I held onto to get me through, something that got erased when he pushed me up against the wall of my cell and raped me raw. No matter how many times I tried to get it back afterwards, to try to keep myself from going insane, it was gone." He pushed off the fence and started to pace the dock, "You used to tell me not to be like them. That they were animals and that I should have some self-respect, but I never listened. But when I got out of the infirmary and the Brotherhood called me over to their table in the cafeteria? I listened then. To every fucking word."

Jesus Christ. What have I done?

Aaron paced faster. "So when that monkey followed us out of the 'O', when he came up to you and I saw how scared you were, I didn't think twice about what I had to do."

"Had to do?" The anger in Bobby's voice surprised him but he kept on. "The truck was running. You could have gotten in and I would have driven away. You baited that kid, Aaron. You wanted him to come out after us. You didn't have to do that to him. You wanted to."

Aaron stepped towards Bobby and he pressed his back against the fence, their faces inches apart. "He laughed, Bobby. When I screamed for help. When I begged him to stop. He laughed and when he was ready to go again, he did." His lips curled under and he sneered, but his chin crinkled and tears fell. "So you're God damned right I wanted to. The real truth, Bobby, straight up? I'm sorry I didn't kill him. Fuck that kid. Fuck my cellmate. Fuck all of them." He backed away towards the door and pointed at Bobby as he went. "And fuck you, too, Bobby. All I did is exactly what you always wanted me to do." He opened the door to back inside.

"You *did* kill him!"

Aaron stopped but kept his back to Bobby. Then he stepped back inside. The door clicked shut behind him.

Bobby didn't realize he'd been holding his breath when Aaron stood in his face. He let it out in a rush and held himself up on his knees. He had fucked everything up without even knowing it. When Isabel told Bobby and Grandpap the truth about his father, she dropped a nuke, but Bobby thought the fallout only affected him. Passing for white never affected anyone else. At least that's what he told himself. Every time he and Aaron got bullied, every insult they wore pushed Bobby deeper into his denial. With Aaron, Bobby wasn't alone anymore. He was almost the perfect friend except he wanted to be everything that Bobby hated about himself, so he shamed Aaron for his wannabe act, never thinking it would leave this thing in him, like a mutant gene just waiting for some event to trigger his evil super power.

But this wasn't a comic book.

It was hard for Bobby to think of Aaron back in jail, but the idea of him murdering that kid coupled with the fact that he had wanted to scared Bobby far more than the idea of what would happen to Aaron if he went back. It frightened him more than the idea that turning Aaron in likely meant jail for him, too. If he had stood up for himself and not gone into the 'O', none of this would have happened. If he'd stayed to help that kid, Aaron would be going to jail and not him. If he'd thrown out Mom's booze instead of making sure she rolled to her side to keep from choking on her own vomit at night, maybe things would have been different for *them*, too. His excuses piled up like so much shit except now he wasn't the only one covered in stench. He needed to get clean, but maybe now he didn't have to do it alone. His father was here, and maybe somehow, he could help him figure out what to do.

Robert would help him.

Bobby walked back to the front of the restaurant. He wanted to keep walking down to the bus stop and go home, help Mom clean up and then sit her down and tell her what happened, so that they could figure a way to tell it to Robert. But they still had rent due and now there was no way he could let her use the money Aaron had given him. He'd find a way to get it back, somehow. At the entrance, the hostesses gave Bobby confused looks while they held open the double doors for him, wondering where he'd come from when he had been inside minutes before. Michelle stood at the bus stand, sorted through checks and counted out change. Bobby walked up to her.

"What the hell, man?" she asked. "You have a nice time? I'm getting slammed and Russell is pissed." She looked up and stopped sorting. "Jesus, are you okay?"

Bobby guessed he didn't look so hot. "Believe it or not," he said, "I'm good." He went through her pile of checks. "Where're we at?"

For the next few hours, Bobby lost himself in work. He and Michelle turned and burned tables, and charmed customers out of their money. Bobby laughed a little, and even managed not to think about things for brief moments. He helped Michelle run food. Aaron was on the fryer, not supervising the line, but even the times Bobby had to take food from his window, he didn't avoid it. He even looked him in the eye. Knowing that he would make this right, that it was almost over, was freeing.

Bobby was afraid about what turning them in could mean for him. He didn't know anything about the law, but he knew driving away from the scene of an assault was going to get him more than a stern talking-to and a wag of the finger. When he thought about ending up where Aaron went—about ending his first week the way Aaron had—Bobby's mouth went dry. As fearful as that made him, for the first time in the last few days, he wasn't afraid of Aaron anymore, and that made him feel the slightest bit better.

The dinner rush ended, and he'd made enough to clear another month's rent, but Bobby wanted more. Michelle was okay with it, so he asked the second and third cuts if they wanted to go home and the two of them took over two more sections. The kitchen made their cuts as well and Bobby saw Aaron seated at the bar with a bottle of Bud and a shot in front of him. He snapped open a Zippo and lit it, then snapped it shut, then repeated, in between gulps of beer. Michelle and Bobby sent the hostesses home and alternated manning the door and seating every table that came in. There weren't many more customers, but every table they took meant more money for Isabel if Bobby went to prison. One less double she'd have to work. Maybe time to go to AA. He'd make her swear to it, jail time or no.

Bobby watched Aaron when it was his turn on the door. He'd counted at least three beers gone in just minutes, and an equal number of empty shot glasses lined the bar until Paul cleared them and poured another. Paul had never liked Aaron much either, and was all too happy to take his money. How shitfaced would he let Aaron get before he cut him off? He saw him driving, swerving into a pole or going off the bridge into the Monongahela. Bobby didn't want Aaron to die, though he knew sending him back to jail might mean just that. It also might mean he'd get help. Bobby would tell the police what happened to Aaron in prison and maybe they'd get him a shrink. Something. The constant back and forth lessened his nerve for this whole thing. The outer doors of the restaurant opened while Bobby bargained with himself, and he pushed open the inside door to greet another table. Darryl walked in with another black young man. Darryl smacked his friend in the chest when he saw Bobby and laughed.

"Here go one of them right here," Darryl said to him. His friend sucked air through his teeth and gave Bobby the same once over Bobby had given him. They walked up to the bar. Darryl pointed out Aaron to his friend when they got to the top and Bobby was scared all over again. If they were here about Aaron, and about what he said about Darryl's cousin, well then maybe Aaron had it coming. But maybe Darryl's cousin had been in on the assaults that took place after the first one. Maybe Aaron took him out for payback. Maybe that wasn't okay.

This night needed to end.

There was an hour left until close.

Aaron hadn't seen Darryl and his friend, or he was too drunk to care. All of Bobby and Michelle's tables had their food, so Bobby joined her as she stood at the bus stand. She cocked her head towards Darryl.

"That looks like trouble," she said.

"It ain't good," Bobby said.

"You think they're here for you and Aaron?"

"Darryl knows the kitchen's closed," Bobby said. "So, I doubt they're here for dinner."

Michelle let out a breath. "Everybody's eating," she said. "I'll go drop the checks." She walked off before Bobby could argue. The tables that didn't pay right away flagged her down by the time she'd brought change and credit slips back to the ones who had. They closed out all their checks soon after that. It had been a good night. Together they made more than Bobby had ever pulled in on a double. He took a twenty from the pile and slid it over to Michelle but she wouldn't take it. Bobby reluctantly pocketed it and looked back to Darryl and his friend. They watched Aaron who looked almost asleep, still seemingly unaware of them. Michelle took off her apron and her baseball hat and ran her fingers through her hair.

"Hot date?" he asked.

"Get your friend and go home," she said. She walked towards Darryl's side of the bar and Bobby reached for her arm. She stopped.

"Why?" he asked. "After what Aaron said to you last night. Jesus, after what I said. You don't owe us anything."

"Because it's hard to do the right thing," she said. "Isn't it?"

"Thank you."

"See you tomorrow, huh? We're a good team."

She walked away and came up behind Darryl and his friend and put her hands on their backs. They turned around in their stools and put their backs to Aaron. Bobby quickly counted out Paul's tip share and joined Aaron at the bar as he ordered another shot from Paul. Paul pulled the tequila bottle from the well while Bobby put his tip share on the counter and gave him the "cut him off" sign. Paul shrugged and replaced the bottle, scooped the money from the bar, and walked away to tend to the others.

"It's time to go, Aaron," Bobby said.

"I'm fine," he mumbled. "Where's my shot?"

"Where are your keys?"

He pointed across the bar to Darryl. "See our boys over there?"

"Yes, Aaron. I see them. Keys? Before they see us."

"I don't know what happened to his cousin, you know."

"What?"

"Darryl's cousin," he said. "I don't even know who he is," he said. "I might have heard his name before. Just said it to piss him off. Think it worked."

"What about the spiderweb tattoo?" Bobby asked. Aaron chugged the rest of his beer and waved to Paul for another, but Bobby held his hand up.

"I didn't mean it," Aaron said. "What happened to him. The kid. I'm not. That's not me. I swear."

Aaron pushed back and his stool fell over but Bobby caught it before it hit the floor. He kept an eye on Darryl, still distracted by Michelle. Aaron stared at Bobby and steadied himself on the bar. Bobby reached out and put the palm of his hand on his cheek and gave it two gentle pats. Aaron's voice shook.

"I couldn't help it. You believe me, right?"

"It's time to go, man," Bobby said.

Aaron scrunched up his mouth and nodded, dug into his pocket, and handed Bobby his keys. His knees buckled and locked as Bobby walked behind him, his hands guarding Aaron at his sides. Across the bar, Michelle and Bobby met eyes for a moment and Darryl turned to see what she saw. Bobby kept his hand at Aaron's back and guided him down the steps and when he looked back, he saw Darryl getting his friend's attention. Bobby didn't look back again and hurried Aaron out the doors into the freezing cold night.

It had started snowing.

The truck roared to life and the back end fishtailed as they merged onto McKnight Road. The hour was late and the traffic sparse. Bobby's eyes shuttled from the road to the rearview. A pair of headlights appeared as pinpricks in the relative darkness over the hill and Bobby's pulse quickened. He slowed the truck to the speed limit and moved to the right lane. The change caused Aaron to shift in his seat, and his head came to rest on the passenger side window. He grunted and reclined his seat, then lay back, open-mouthed. The dots of light grew larger and brighter, more quickly than Bobby wanted, until they were within ten feet of his bumper. His foot pressed the accelerator. He'd meant to stay slow, hoping they'd pass, but fear took hold. The truck pulled away and the car flashed its high beams. The traffic light ahead went yellow, but Bobby's terror granted him brief clarity of thought, and he realized that speeding increased his chances of getting pulled over, which made his story go from the truth of a confession to the excuse of someone who'd just been caught. He slowed to a stop. A heavy bass track thumped as the other car stopped behind them.

CHAPTER
EIGHTEEN

After she had left Robert and Bobby, Isabel waited until she got in the car and locked the door. Then she screamed. Then she cried, hard. Then she laughed as she hugged herself tight until she let it all out, until her stomach ached, and her throat felt raw. When all that was done, she drove home.

She turned up the radio on the way. She usually left it off; the signal was weak, filled with static such that she could never find a good channel, but she needed a soundtrack for her celebratory drive home. The jazz station played an upbeat Miles Davis number and she turned it up as loud as she could stand. Then she realized that she still didn't like jazz. It had been just another thing of which she'd convinced herself when it came to Robert, even after all these years. She laughed as she snapped off the music and tapped her hands on the wheel to a random, meandering tune that she composed as she went. When thought about how happy she was, she felt surprise when she realized she was truly happy, though not for herself.

Robert would fall in love with Bobby as hard as she had. He'd want to be a father to him, and Bobby would want him as his father. There would be questions, so many questions, some regret, maybe even some anger, but when they could get past all those necessary things, they could get on with the business of father and son. It occurred to her more than once on the drive that Bobby might not need her anymore, but then he hadn't for a long time. The way he spoke to her before she left made her think that it wasn't even a matter of need, but want. If he decided to go, to somehow leave with Robert and start again, well, then he deserved that. They both did. And that would be all right.

Bobby wouldn't be home for hours and the apartment looked like hell. Isabel guessed it always had, but tonight she saw things in a much harsher light. She didn't know why, but she wanted the house to be perfect when Bobby came home. The nozzle of the tile cleaner had crusted over from disuse and the window cleaning fluid dried to a blue film at the bottom of the spray bottle. She unscrewed the cap and pressed out a few drops of gel and scrubbed the counters with a mildewed rag they had tied around the pipes to the kitchen faucet to keep them from leaking. Swept the linoleum, scrubbed the tub, wiped down the refrigerator shelves, made the bed, took out the trash.

Tried to polish shit and hoped it didn't smell.

She opened the freezer, forgetting she'd finished off the last bottle of vodka the first night she ran into Robert, so she went to the cabinet and took down the jelly jar and counted out thirty bucks. Just thirty. They were so close on the rent and Bobby was working tonight. They deserved to celebrate. Maybe he'd even have one drink with her. Tomorrow they'd all toast each other. Isabel started for the door, then stopped. The money wasn't right. Had she miscounted?

She went through the cash again and there was more than enough for one month's rent. Had he picked up more time without telling her? Christ, had he taken on another job?

What are you doing, Izzy? You want to celebrate? You want to pretend any booze you buy's going to be for anyone but you? No. You're sabotaging this whole thing, that's what, and I know it's what you do but you have to stop that now. At least tonight. At least for tomorrow. Give this, give Bobby, give them *the chance they deserve. You think Bobby's going to forgive you if you're drunk and stumbling over your own tongue? Don't you do it. Don't you fuck this up for him. Who are you celebrating for?*

"For him," she said.

Isabel walked back to the kitchen and put the money away, then walked down the hall to the bedroom and climbed under the tightly pulled sheets. Her pictures of the two of them were still in the nightstand and she took them out and held them to her chest. It had been almost a full day without a drink again. She closed her eyes and tried to ignore the throbbing in her head.

CHAPTER
NINETEEN

A car horn blew at Robert at every red light that turned green. He couldn't focus. He worried he wouldn't be up for the long hours and wondered if he would be competent enough for even an hour of work, let alone talking to Marcus's parents after their son had just died. The last thing they needed was to hear any kind of news from a doctor whose head wasn't in the game. And his head was most certainly not in the game. After another missed green light and another angry beep, Robert pulled off Fifth and put the car in park. He turned off the radio and replayed the last twenty-four hours in his head.

When Izzy first told him he was her son, he'd been furious. He'd gone back to work right after the miscarriage, and it had been too soon. He and Tamara were more than comfortable financially; they could have afforded to have them both be home, but the house, for all its extravagance felt crushing. Tamara folded in on herself and

Robert had no one else. He'd prepare meals for her day, pack them in glass containers in the fridge and then make his escape.

He and Tamara had spent thousands on tests, changed their diets, their sleep cycles. Robert switched to boxers and stopped hot showers. They set timers for sex and only in certain positions depending on where she was in her cycle, definitely not twice in a row and certainly not after drinking. They had gotten so clinical about conception that as a couple, they had gone sterile. It was no wonder they fell apart after the miscarriage. There was simply nothing left of them.

Robert and his father often argued at length about the ways Robert wasn't "black enough," and how, to Robert, his father's version of black just meant fulfilling the stereotype he was expected to occupy and how he would never do that. Pledge Kappas, Omegas, Sigmas, catch a whooping by your own people in the name of brotherhood, with all the dignity of an oversized wooden paddle, when our people died escaping from beatings. Spin that cane and step, shuffle those feet, show those teeth. Dance, nigger, dance. Keep it real.

How could you want me to do that? he'd asked him.

Yet here he was, another brother with a white girl telling him he was a daddy.

Wouldn't his father be proud?

He argued with himself about all the reasons he should walk away while he could. But he couldn't be like the brothers who shamed him, the type he and Tamara would deride over drinks about the way they had been mocked by them, both as they grew up and even as adults. He wouldn't be the punch line to some joke white people looked over both shoulders before telling.

Marcus' parents had only spoken to the neurosurgeon and the attending. Robert felt a pang of guilt at having been spared "the talk." Though he was well practiced at it, he had failed to summon the callous he would have needed this time. This case in particular felt too close to home. His emotions too high.

The rest of the night in the ER was unmercifully slow. It was an evening of lingering colds, mystery pains and burning urination, with gaps of too much time to think in between. Robert looked at the same page of the same chart for a half an hour, searching not for information, but for the answers. *Where did this put him with Isabel? Would he owe child support? Would Bobby want to live with him? Would Robert want him to live with him?*

He closed the chart and went on to the next patient with the hopes for answers in the light of the next day.

CHAPTER
TWENTY

She awakened to pure blackness. The pulsing in her temples converted to pounding. She despised drying out. She switched on the light on her nightstand and sat on the edge of the bed and wished for the mercy of a hangover headache, far more forgiving than a sober one. It was after two in the morning. The excitement of the day had taken it out of her and she couldn't believe she'd slept that long. Bobby would be asleep on the couch and she knew she should let him rest, but she couldn't wait until morning to talk to him about what he and Robert had said. Sleep when you're dead, she'd tell him when she couldn't get him up for school.

No light in the hallway. No lights in the living room, except an orange glow from the streetlight that came in from the window cut-out in the cinderblock where the wall met the ceiling. Isabel hand-walked her way down the hall until her eyes adjusted and she sat on the arm of the couch. When she reached for Bobby's leg, it wasn't there. His pillow still sat on his folded blanket.

Bobby wouldn't touch a drink. He worried that Isabel had passed on more to him in her genes than the curls in her hair, so he was never, ever, out late. He never wanted to spend the money, never when rent was due, or any other time, either. She stood to turn the lights on, to go call the restaurant, hoping he was somehow still there. Maybe some table camped out in his section after closing and refused to pay the check. But this late?

Before she made it to the switch, the room filled with red and blue from the dome lights of a police car traveling slowly down the street. It was nothing unusual in this neighborhood, at this hour, but Isabel felt pressure in her chest and her arms felt heavy and she couldn't pick up the phone.

The car continued its crawl past their window.

Still she couldn't pick up the phone. She wouldn't turn on her lights until theirs went away, but they never went away. They lit the room a little less as they moved further past the window, and then stayed flashing until they stopped.

Shut off. Not faded away.

They had parked.

She told them no.

In the dark of the kitchen every sound reverberated like an explosion. The white noise from the off-air television next door, the refrigerator kicking on, the closing of one car door outside. Then another. The sound of her breathing, the rush of blood in her ears, the sound of footsteps in the hall, too slow to be an emergency, too slow to go past her door. The gentle knock that said they weren't there for *her*, but they were *there* for her.

She told them no.

CHAPTER
TWENTY-ONE

Bobby stared at the halogen headlights in the rearview, the glare left orange spots floating across his vision when he looked away. The muffled bass vibrated through the truck, into his chest, but fell far behind the rhythm of his heart. The driver gunned the engine, then laid on the horn.

Aaron sat up, sleepy-eyed. "Light's green, dude."

Bobby hadn't seen it. He took his foot from the brake and the car revved its engine again before taking a sharp turn around the truck and tore down McKnight road, their taillights leaving a comet-like trail until they disappeared into the night. Bobby placed his foot back on the brake, half expecting the car to turn around at any minute, to see Darryl and his friend through the tinted windshield. But the street remained empty, save another car that passed Bobby on the left and honked.

"What's your problem?" Aaron asked, slurred and irritated.

Bobby put his hand up in apology and passed under the now yellow light and proceeded down the road. He laughed to himself.

Thank you, Michelle.

Aaron moved in and out of consciousness on the drive, the restless sleep of the stone cold drunk. Bobby suspected Aaron didn't share the same feeling of freedom Bobby did from their respective revelations. He alternated looks from the road to Aaron and back again. He seemed so calm in his relative slumber, his shoulders relaxed, the lines in his jaw faded, the anger at bay, at least for the moment. He wondered if he ever truly slept since that first night in prison. It occurred to him that he might not remember the way back to Cort's. He had driven in such a heightened state of fear, he hoped his body would remember. How different this drive seemed from that one. Now that the threat of Darryl and his friend had passed, Bobby felt a sense of serenity that the path that awaited him would be of his choosing.

That this night would not end like that one.

The streets of Oakland were empty once again, and Bobby couldn't ignore the sense of déjà vu, though this feeling had meaning and reason, the memory concrete, not a whisper of a residual of the events of someone else's past life, though many times it felt that way in the hours and days that followed. He ignored the Original as they passed and looked to see if Aaron took notice of where they were, but his head remained back against the rest, lolling with each bump in the road. Bobby saw just past him that the patrol car across from the police station was lit from the inside where there sat two officers. He resisted the urge to speed up.

He made the light. No one followed.

Minutes later, Bobby slowed as he approached a stop sign at the corner of Cort's street. He looked right and accelerated into the turn, but as he looked left, he slammed his foot to the brake. Parked out in front of Cort's apartment sat two patrol cars, dome lights flashing. Bobby's elbows locked and he gripped the steering wheel as four officers headed towards the apartment building. Bobby turned to wake Aaron and flinched back in his seat when he saw Aaron was already upright, eyes wide and glaring at Bobby.

"What did you do?" he asked.

"Aaron, I swear, this wasn't me. The newspaper. They said there were cameras. Security tapes."

"Go straight. Slowly."

"Aaron."

Aaron opened the glove compartment and retrieved the .45. "I said drive."

"Jesus fucking Christ, okay, okay," Bobby said. He eased off the brake and slowly crossed the intersection, eyeing the cops until they were out of his view. He made it to the end of the block and heard no sirens, no screeching tires.

"Turn here," Aaron said.

Bobby pulled on the steering wheel, and as he rounded the corner, he glanced at the rearview mirror and saw a patrol car at the end of the block they'd left behind.

"Shit, shit, shit, shit," Bobby said.

Aaron turned to look out the rear window and cursed. He curled in on himself and squeezed his head between his hands, the .45 in one, and groaned. He smacked the stock of the gun against his forehead.

"Why?" he said. "Why would you do this?"

"Aaron, I swear to fucking God this wasn't me. I swear!"

The patrol car, now behind them, turned on their roof lights and the siren let out a single whoop. The officer called from his speaker.

"Driver, pull over!"

Bobby jumped at the sound and complied. The flashing lights

lit the inside of the truck. Seconds passed like years until the officer ordered them to roll down their windows and place both hands outside. Bobby reached for his door and Aaron growled.

"Don't you touch that fucking button."

Bobby raised his hands and placed them on the wheel, his palms slick with sweat. Aaron looked down at the gun in his hands and spoke in a whisper.

"Why? Why would you do this to me? To us? Do you know what happens if I go back? Do you have any idea what they'll do to *you*?"

"Aaron, listen to what I'm telling you, I swear to you this was not me. I didn't do this." He looked at his driver's side mirror. Both doors of the cruiser opened and the officers perched their arms on the top, guns drawn. "Oh, fuck, Aaron. Jesus, they've got their guns out, man. Please, just turn yourself in."

Aaron opened the glove compartment, pulled back the magazine and shoved it into the stock with a click. Bobby's vocal cords nearly strangled the words in his throat. If he opened the door, the cops would shoot him or Aaron would.

"Aaron, please, don't do this, please, please. They're going to shoot us, man. I don't want to die."

Aaron broke into hysterical sobs. He cradled the gun in both hands. A tear hit the barrel and he wiped it away as he took a deep breath. Bobby looked in the mirror again and saw the cops creeping towards the truck.

"Aaron, put that fucking thing away, they're going to kill us!"

"No, they won't. I'm sorry, Bobby. I love you."

Aaron pressed the barrel to Bobby's eye. It was cold.

Thunder clapped in the cab of the truck. A white light accompanied the high-pitched squeal in Bobby's ears. His face felt wet but he couldn't bring his hands up to wipe it. Nothing would move. The flash-bulb glare faded, as did all other light in the truck.

Bobby watched Aaron open his mouth, saw the cords and muscles in his neck go taut and rigid. He screamed, but the pressure in Bobby's ears muffled the sound.

As the black edges around Bobby's vision swelled, he saw Aaron put the .45 in his mouth.

Bobby heard another report from the gun echo in the cab and Aaron's head snapped back.

The edges closed in.

CHAPTER
TWENTY-TWO

Morning brought no answers, only more questions. Robert's anxiety had reached tsunami heights. At every traffic light, he thought about taking the corner and making the turns that would take him back home to Sewickley, but not Homewood. He kept on. He knew the block of Frankstown where Isabel had told him she lived. Driving it now for the first time struck Robert with a sadness he found difficult to bear. Cars were parked fender to fender, but the block looked abandoned, minutes from where his family home was. His Mama created a world for them to protect them from this one. The lawn, such as it was, was always trimmed and the flower box outside the window was always full of petunias. A garden in the back, no bigger than a sidewalk square, grew okra that she fried and filled the house with smells that felt like warm hands on Robert's face when he came home from school. But the minute he could, Robert ran, off to college and left his Mama to this blight just minutes from her doorstep while she fought to keep that world out. All the while, a boy, her grandson, a child trying to find his way to being a man in the middle of all this, had a world that could have protected him just blocks away. Robert parked the car.

The hallway to Isabel's apartment smelled like abandonment and the condition of the walls and floor reflected the scent. A television blared at full volume. Robert stood in front of her door and knocked. He smoothed the front of his shirt and wiped at the corners of his mouth. He was actually nervous, and he thought about what might be the appropriate greeting when about to sit and talk with your son about the decades passed between them. The light through the peephole remained constant and Robert knocked louder. He began to feel foolish, and more than a bit angry.

She wasn't here.

Was this a con? Had he been manipulated and forced to relive memories he'd tried hard to leave buried?

He repeatedly smacked his open palm on the door. "Isabel!"

The door behind him opened and a greasy-haired white man in sweatpants and an undersized white t-shirt appeared, grayish brown at the armpits. He eyed Robert with suspicion.

"You want to keep it down? Been nothing but noise from that apartment all day," he said.

"Noise? What do you mean?" Robert asked.

"Late last night, or early this morning, however you want to look at it. Screaming woke me right up."

"Was it Isabel?"

"That her name? I guess, yeah. Looked out my door and there's the cops."

Robert pinched the bridge of his nose. This had been some kind of scam. "Arresting her?" he asked.

"Not that I could tell, because next thing I know there's two

EMT's taking her out on a stretcher. Wailing something awful."

A heaviness settled in Robert's chest.

"Hope she's all right," the man continued. "Just kept saying 'no,' over and over again."

This was no con, Robert thought. She hadn't been caught in some scheme. Jesus, what had happened?

"Where was her son?"

"I didn't see anybody but her."

Robert thanked him and ran down the hallway. Back to his car, Robert pulled out onto Frankstown and drove as fast as he could to the only other place someone might know where to find her.

Lou's was closed, but through the glass door, Robert saw Nico behind the counter slicing lemons. Robert slapped his hand against the glass and Nico looked up. His expression when he saw Robert was not the same as the night before. The disdain remained but something else circled the borders of it. He unlocked the door and let Robert in. As Robert took a stool, Nico folded his arms and leaned against the countertop behind him.

"Look, I know you don't like me, all right?" Robert said. "I don't know why, but I've got my guesses. I don't know what Izzy has or hasn't told you, but I can tell you that unless you talked to her since last night, a lot of it probably isn't what you think. I'm asking you, please, if you know where she is, tell me what happened."

Nico crossed his arms across his stomach and let out a breath through pursed lips.

"We met yesterday, me, Izzy, and Bobby," Robert continued. We were supposed to talk again today. I went to their apartment but neither of them were there. Bobby told me had to take care of something. Does this have something to do with that?"

Nico pulled a rocks glass from the bar and placed it front of Robert. Robert said no, but Nico pulled a bottle of Glen Fiddich from the shelf and poured generously.

"Believe me," he said. "You'll want a drink."

Robert took a sip while Nico rested his forearms on the bar and told Robert the story he said the police had told him.

Robert stared past him at his own reflection in the spotted mirror lining the wall behind the bar.

"There had been an assault two nights ago," said Nico. "Turns out it was that tattooed behemoth in the truck with Bobby. Put a brick through the face of some kid outside the Original in Oakland."

Oh, my God. The kid in the ICU.

"The whole thing got caught on a security tape," Nico said. "According to the cops, someone else was there, because this muscle-headed freak jumped in the passenger side of a red pickup and they took off like a shot. The camera footage was kind of grainy and they couldn't see through the glare on the windshield to tell who was driving, but they picked up a part of the license plate. The cops tried to talk to the other guy, the one with the kid that got all fucked up—"

"He's dead," Robert said.

"Oh, shit," Nico said. "That sucks. Anyway, the guy wouldn't talk to the cops. Even to help out his boy. Ain't that something?"

Robert glared at Nico, but he seemed not to notice.

"Anyway, the plates come up belonging to this other guy, out on parole. The police find out the address of where he's staying from his P.O. and send two squad cars. The cops are just getting out to walk up to the apartment when—don't you know—that red pick-up shows up." Nico poured himself a drink and took a sip.

"Did they think Bobby was driving the night of the assault?" Robert asked.

"It's all a guess at this point. But yeah, probably."

Robert shook his head as if to shake loose the story. Bobby had embraced him so warmly when they'd met. Was it possible he was capable of something like this? Did he have that kind of hate in his heart?

"Why did he drive away?" Robert asked. "Why would he leave that kid there to die?"

"Bobby was a good kid, man. Before you go casting judgment."

"That's not what I meant."

"Shit, he was probably scared, man. Twenty-something-year-old kid probably never saw anything like that in his life. Imagine you're seeing that horror show. I'd have hauled ass, too."

They let out simultaneous breaths in a whoosh.

"Where's Isabel now?" Robert asked. "A man in her building said they took her out of the apartment screaming."

"You're a doctor, right?" Nico asked. "What's that number when they take you away for cracking up?"

"Three zero two."

Nico snapped his fingers. "That's the one. Yeah, they three-oh-two'd her to the psych ward at county. Probably best, too. If she's going to deal with this, she's going to need to stay dried out and get it together. That kid was all she had. He didn't like me much, but he took care of her when she couldn't take care of herself." Robert thought he heard a crack in his voice. Nico saw Robert watching him and cleared his throat. "Anyway, she'll stay with me when she gets out."

Robert put his head in his hands. "Jesus Christ," he said.

Nico raised his drink and gestured for Robert to do the same, and they touched glasses.

"Amen to that," Nico said. "Let me ask you something now."

Robert looked up and nodded.

"After Isabel woke up in the ward," Nico said, "she started talking to me about Bobby's dad."

Robert swallowed hard and looked back down into his glass,

swirling the cubes.

"She kept talking about how Bobby had met him. She was still pretty doped up at that point, and as far as I knew, Bobby's dad was dead, so it actually made sense to me, you know? Them finally getting to meet and what not. I thought it was the saddest fucking thing I'd ever heard, but I understood it." He finished his pint and rinsed it in the sink. "But then you show up here today, after appearing out of nowhere just a couple of days ago." He put the glass on the drying rack and stood in front of Robert again, arms folded. "She was talking about you, huh?"

All of Robert's swirling melted the ice and the outside of the glass sweated. Nico looked as if he already knew the answer, waiting for Robert to say it.

"Yes," Robert said.

An overwhelming sense of dread, one that had started in Robert's stomach in front of Isabel's apartment door, expanded until it compressed everything inside and pushed his heart up against his ribs until each beat resonated through his bones. And when Nico told him that Bobby was dead, he wanted to find some way to tell Tamara he was sorry. He finally understood. In some ways he'd never taken possession of the child they lost. Because she'd carried it, she knew it in a way he couldn't. She shared a feeling with the baby that was just between them and though Robert didn't know it then, he resented them both for it. But in that moment, he knew without a doubt that Bobby was his, because for a brief instant when Nico said he was gone, Robert felt like he wanted to die.

"Crazy how much he looked like you," Nico said. "White as he was. Can't believe I didn't see it before, but then I guess I wasn't really looking."

Tears rolled down Robert's cheeks.

Robert took a deep breath and wiped at his eyes. "What can I do?"

Nico's shoulders relaxed and his face softened. He leaned his elbows on the bar.

"Stay away from her. She sees you, she sees him."

Robert closed his eyes and balled his fists. He wanted to grab Nico by the collar of his shirt and drag him across the bar for being territorial in this moment, but something in what he said resonated. He thought of Tamara again and wondered if that must have been what she felt—that each time she looked at him, she was reminded of what they had lost.

He opened his hands, placed them on the bar, and stood.

"Please tell her I'm sorry," Robert said. He reached in his jacket for his wallet, but Nico dismissed the gesture and patted his chest to tell Robert they were on him. Robert copied his movement as a thank you and looked back once as he walked out. Nico gave a single nod of his head and resumed his prep work for the day ahead.

Outside it felt a little warmer than it had earlier in the day, but the wind shot down the streets in frigid gusts. Large flakes fell from the ash-grey sky and thunder rumbled in the distance. They predicted another squall coming through, the last leg of the nor'easter as it swirled over Pittsburgh and made its way up the states. Robert walked back to his car in a daze. He felt outside of himself, but not just watching him. He watched it all, from some other place in time where all of their lives drove on separate streets, running in parallel at first, but converging on a point. When he got in and closed the door behind him, those lives came together, cars all trying to beat the light at an intersection and colliding.

Robert cried, harder than he'd ever cried in his life, for all of them, everyone all at once, and when he was done, he started the car and drove home.

Acknowledgments

I begin with the usual disclaimer that if there is someone I've forgotten, please know that any omission is not intentional. There have been so many who have been exceedingly generous with their time, love, counsel, and support, that it's quite easy to lose track. It's a good problem to have.

To my editor, Chantelle Osman, I am eternally grateful that you saw something in this story and took a chance on it and me. At the sake of sounding cliché, I could not have asked for a better or more patient editor, and I look forward to working with you for a long time to come.

To my publisher, Jason Pinter. I sincerely appreciate your vision in bringing Agora to life, and in trusting me to be a part of the inaugural class. Here's to a long and lasting partnership!

Michelle Richter, my agent, you made the leap with me and I couldn't be more thankful. Here's to more deals in the future.

Paula Munier, my story would never have gotten to where it had without your valuable input and advice. I hope our paths continue to cross on our respective writing journeys.

Mom and Dad, it took me a while to figure out what I was meant to do, but with your support, I did it. I love you both.

Ted Flanagan. My homeboy. Ever since the first day of the MFA program, we've been fast friends, and now the best of friends. Not only that, but you're my most trusted second reader, sounding board, and therapist when the impostor syndrome rears its ugly head. The day we're doing panels and readings together is fast approaching. Thank you for being there every step of the way. May your head ever bobble.

Diane Les Becquets, Richard Carey, thank you for seeing something in my writing. One phone call changed the direction of my life.

Merle Drown, Chinelo Okparanta, and Mitch Wieland, thank you for your guidance and sharing your wisdom, friendship, and knowledge of the craft. I would not have found my voice without you.

Gabino Iglesias and Matt Coleman, your early and continued support for a random guy you met on Twitter continues to amaze me. I'm proud to call you friends and to be a part of your community.

Big shout out goes to Kellye Garrett and the rest of the Crime Writers of Color community, which is getting too large to name everyone, and that's a damn good thing.

Thank you to the crew at Cognoscenti, namely Kelly Horan, Frannie Carr Toth, and Kathleen Burge. You gave my words a voice and a forum and I will never forget it.

Bob Shaffer and Sharon Brody at WBUR Boston, meeting you both and having the opportunity to work with you was one of the most memorable experiences of my life. I am indebted to both of you for the opportunity you provided me.

Finally, Michelle Vercher. Your unwavering love and support for this dream pushed me through so many periods of self-doubt and insecurity. You are my best friend, my partner-in-crime, an incredible mother, and the best wife a man can hope for. I can't imagine a day where laughter doesn't fill the rooms of our home. I cheese sandwich you, Peanut.

About the Author

John Vercher is a writer currently living in the Philadelphia area with his wife and two sons. He holds a Bachelor's in English from the University of Pittsburgh and an MFA in Creative Writing from the Mountainview Master of Fine Arts program. His fiction has appeared on Akashic Books' Mondays are Murder and Fri-SciFi. and he is a contributing writer for Cognoscenti, the thoughts and opinions page of WBUR Boston. Two of his essays published there on race, identity, and parenting were picked up by NPR, and he has appeared on WBUR's Weekend Edition. His non-fiction has also appeared in Entropy Magazine. You can find him on his website www.johnvercherauthor.com and on Twitter at @jverch75.

CPSIA information can be obtained
at www.ICGtesting.com
Printed in the USA
LVHW090043081119
636695LV00001B/1/P